THE
WHO WENT

For Denny Graubart, the chaotic summer of 1967, when the screams of napalm bombs drowned the cheers of the All-Star game, brings the painful realisation that childhood has passed. Engaging in his favourite domestic spying game, Denny unwittingly discovers the desperate measures his mother will take to save his autistic brother Fad in the diagnostic Dark Ages of the 1960s.

At the heart of this dark and funny first novel is not only the story of Denny's reluctant entrance to adolescence, but also that of his relationship with Fad, whose departure from 44 Drainer Drive at the end of the summer will forever alter both their lives.

ELI GOTTLIEB

Eli Gottlieb was born in New York City and raised in New Jersey. He has taught American literature at the University of Padua, Italy, written documentary films, and worked as a senior editor at *Elle* magazine. In 1998 Eli Gottlieb was awarded the prestigious Prix de Rome by the American Academy of Arts and Letters for *The Boy Who Went Away*. He currently lives in upstate New York.

Eli Gottlieb

THE BOY WHO WENT AWAY

V

VINTAGE

Published by Vintage 1998

2 4 6 8 10 9 7 5 3 1

Portions of this book were originally published in
slightly different form in *Conjunctions* magazine

First published in Great Britain by
Jonathan Cape 1997

Vintage
Random House, 20 Vauxhall Bridge Road,
London SW1V 2SA

Random House Australia (Pty) Limited
20 Alfred Street, Milsons Point, Sydney
New South Wales 2061, Australia

Random House New Zealand Limited
18 Poland Road, Glenfield,
Auckland 10, New Zealand

Random House South Africa (Pty) Limited
Endulini, 5A Jubilee Road, Parktown 2193,
South Africa

Random House UK Limited Reg. No. 954009

A CIP catalogue record for this book
is available from the British Library

ISBN 0 09 978061 5

Papers used by Random House UK Ltd are natural,
recyclable products made from wood grown in sustain-
able forests. The manufacturing processes conform to the
environmental regulations of the country of origin

Printed and bound in Great Britain by
Cox & Wyman, Reading, Berkshire

For my brother Joshua, and for Danella

CONTENTS

THE BOY

WHO

WENT

AWAY

JUNE

ONE

I first noticed something strange happening to my mother six months earlier, in the motionless days of January. During a cold snap that turned everything the hue of smoke, her clothes suddenly began to grow bright, vivid, as if powered by a secret store of summer brilliance. Although it was frigid outside, her skirts shrank upward above the knees, while the heels of her shoes grew downward into spikes curved like the teeth of animals that made a racketing, military clatter on the floors of our house. I was sick with the flu for two weeks straight, and I noticed that with my father gone to work for the day, she would sometimes go upstairs and spend an hour carefully penciling freshness into her face—and then, to my amazement, leave on a long "run to the store." She seemed energized at strange times of the day, sparked into excited conversation by a random headline, a snatch of music on the Magnavox, or the blue of two jays she'd spotted tussling over seeds in the snow of our backyard. Bouncing as she walked, she would sometimes, for no obvious reason, come up to me and interrupt what I was doing to ask, "Front and center, sweetness, how *are* you?"

As time went on, I couldn't help but notice that the

energy in Harta's face and her newly brisk stride seemed to correspond to a deepening fatigue in my father, Max. As she bloomed, he shrank, cutting his household functions back to the minimum, and skirting the family whenever possible. Every morning, dressed in a blue suit, he ate an egg, inspected the rattling panes of *The New York Times,* swept out of the house trailing an extravagant scarf of aftershave, and said the following words: yes, no, perhaps. Every evening, home from work, he flung open the front door, stood unsteadily a moment surveying us with slitted eyes, and then went silently to his basement workshop, trailing a yeasty fog of alcohol. One night he moved his bar down there. A television followed. For six nights in a row he took his supper down there, too.

It seemed to me there had to be a connection between these two different states, one parent rising, the other falling, like a seesaw ridden by formally dressed adults. Several months went by, while I kept my thoughts to myself, watched and waited, carefully noted all small signs of change and disturbance of household routine. As my surveillance notebooks swelled, the disproportion in my parents' happiness seemed only to grow larger.

On June 7, the last day of school, Mr. Davies, the balding principal, gathered us for an assembly in the auditorium to formally announce that school was over. He clapped his hands, Ed Stankiewicz blew something fancy on a trumpet, and the old janitor, Peterson, threw open the steel doors and went to have his millionth cigarette of the day. I walked out, dazed and blinking into the light, and went slowly home. I was happy school was over—very happy, maybe even a little sick with happiness—but mainly I was looking forward to putting into motion what I'd been planning for several weeks. The very next morning, I woke up bright and early, stuffed a shopping bag full of all the surveillance material I'd collected on my family over the previous half-year, and snuck out the back door to see my friend and adviser Derwent Prine.

Derwent and his family lived six houses down the hill from us, in a small split-level that always smelled slightly used. This was a tired, sour smell, like standing flower water. Because Derwent was a genius, I took great comfort from the fact that we lived higher up on the hill than he did, closer to the sky, to the stars at night, and to the bald, wandering eye of the moon, whose beams were lashes and whose pupil, rocky and dilated, was a crater the size of Minnesota.

"The Gulf of Tonkin is a lie," I stated into the air of Derwent's living room that afternoon. I was addressing Derwent's mother, who sat in front of me with her hair gathered and radiating backward like a fanlight from the center of her forehead. Mrs. Prine leaned forward, interested. I attempted to cast a mild glance up her skirt, where the darkness intervened.

"Would you like some cookies?" she said.

"Na."

She was wearing her nursing clothes, because that's what she did, she nursed.

I coughed importantly, and made a vague shape in the air with my hands.

"Derwent coming home soon?"

"Any minute," she said in a cheery voice.

There was a disturbance at the door—a click, and an extended whine. The big calf of a leg entered the room, followed by shorts, a stained T-shirt, and a head of girlishly long hair, parted in the middle.

"Hey," said Derwent, slinging his bag onto the floor.

"Denny's been here to see you and we've been chatting," said his mother brightly.

"C'm'ere, Clausewitz," said Derwent, ignoring her.

I got up, went over. "Bar the nannygoat from the door," Derwent said, and winked. His mother froze. I looked at her out of the corner of my eye, and she was perfectly frozen with her hands in the air and a cheerful, easy smile balanced on her face.

"I told you to never drop in unannounced," he whispered fiercely, drawing me by the lapels up the stairs. We turned the corner into the carpeted hallway.

"It's important," I said.

"It better be," Derwent muttered, leading me into his room, a space that continued the atmospheric theme of the house, smelling dankly fatigued, deprived of essential oxygen. I imagined ferns in the corners, wigs of moss climbing the walls, and fish, perhaps, sitting glumly in bowls of water beneath the beds.

"Actually," said Derwent, sitting down on a stool, "you're a very lucky guy."

"How so?" I asked.

"You're going to be the first person to get the news. As of yesterday, I can officially say I've got the lowdown on Daddy-o."

"Your father?"

"Natch, numbnuts. You know my dad's briefcase?"

"Sure, what about it?"

"Whaddya think is in it?"

"I dunno." I shrugged. "Reports of some kind?" His father was an industrial chemist. "Equations?"

Derwent, who was rumored to have the highest IQ in Essex County, got up and began pacing rapidly to and fro. After a moment he turned, strode up to me, and shot a triumphant look my way—which caused me, irresistibly, to look out the window. I gazed away from Derwent and his heavy-water brain and stared out at the backyard, whose grass was the same scuffed spearmint shade as our own. In the center of the yard his mother was hanging the wash on the wires of their four-way doohickey, and as I watched, she reached upward and the wind, working, blew her hair up over her head and flattened her shift against her breasts. My blood jumped.

"Porn," said Derwent. "Snatch, cooze, the real stuff."

It took a moment for the words to register.

"Do you mean—" I began thickly, but he cut me off.

"In spades, frodo. Dad is not the devout factor we've taken him for. He's a filthy-minded little bastard, a schmuck and most likely a philanderer too. I bet he takes it in his fist on the uptown bus!"

"Wow," I said, understanding the general drift, but not the details. "But how could—" I stopped. "What do you want to do about it?"

Derwent nodded soberly, reached under the bed on which I was sitting, and with a tiny confident twitch of the head, as if underlining a point in conversation, drew the briefcase out between my feet.

"Vwah-lah!" he said, but softly.

"Is this it?" I was somewhat incredulous.

"In point of fact, yes. What I've saved for your arrival was the official opening. I need an official witness. I'm thinking of drawing up papers allowing me legal control of my future. If you're willing to go to court with me, I think I can nail Dad on Statute 11–17. Endangering the welfare of a minor. But as I say, I need your assistance."

He clicked open the locks, and slowly, almost tenderly, opened the case.

Colors bloomed. A big sunburst of reds and oranges flew out into the air. I stared, goggling, as these colors resolved for a moment into violins and grapefruit, gulls and pantries. And from there, presently, into the bodies of women.

I blinked. I had peeked into such magazines before, of course. At the pharmacy or stationery store I had parted the pages of *Playboy* and gazed at torsos, which seemed like so much baker's dough, freshly risen into the rounded perfection of curve balls and planetary orbits. These *Playboy* women had been demure; they were carefully airbrushed below the waist. They provoked in me a burning curiosity about the critical bit of underworld where their thighs met and where something was located, I knew, something incredibly complementary of what stuck out of the center of my own body. We would *dock* somehow, I figured. But I was uncertain as to the details.

Until now. I gazed at the copies of *Beaver* and *Raunch* and *Slut* and I beheld women with crushed, desperately smiling faces, and all at once, to the accompaniment of a chord of music, I dropped my eye and understood.

Good God!

Everything I'd been told was true! These little coral hoops at the centers of their bodies, these mustachioed pink mouths with the wetness of throats to them—they were for swallowing us! Women swallowed food from above, and men from below!

Or was it vice versa?

"Yer basic meatus," said Derwent, who was two years older than I. He got up and closed the door.

"Geesh," I said, and stared. The women all had expressions on their faces of tasting something shockingly good, or of seeing the moment in the movies, perhaps, when the Girl and the Guy meet in a deep, drinking kiss. They seemed ecstatic for no particular reason. Their hands were often in the air, bodies bent in postures meant, I understood dimly, to suggest abandon. And there were those faces, slashed open at the mouth, slit-eyed and wanton at the same time. Some of them had their hands at the top of their—I said the word slowly in my mind—*vaginas,* while others had put their fingers inside, as if to retrieve a piece of food stuck between two teeth.

"A frigging windfall," said Derwent, in a voice of masterful calm. "A goddamn treasure trove."

Something began to blink, then. A tiny dart of curiosity shot through me.

"This is amazing, but I gotta ask you a question," I said.

"Yeah? What."

"Uhn, like what does your dad do with it?"

Derwent began to smile, and then the smile grew into something bigger than a smile, and then he flat-out began to laugh—a hooting, repetitive cackle that showed off his teeth. Tetracycline allergies had left them covered with yellow spots, like leaf blight. He stopped laughing and shook his head.

"You're a regular scream," he said. "Whuddya think he does?"

"That's what I'm asking."

"Naw." Derwent made a face of doubt, which presently unscrambled itself. "You're not shitting me?"

"No, I'm serious."

"Sometimes, pal, you amaze even me. Okay, let's begin at the beginning. What Pops does is, he looks at the stuff, and then he more or less takes his dowel in his hand and then pulls on it until—until, what, he blows his wad of course! Is that enough for you?"

Very vaguely, I got the idea.

"Your dad does *that?*" I remembered the grave, dignified expression his father had, which seemed to imply that at any given moment, in a deeply sober voice, he might ask you to pass the gravy boat. High school principals had such expressions. Men discussing the president on television had it.

Policemen had it. The thought that such men likewise reached into their flies, took out their peckers, and in their individual households waxed them like the blades of skates was the equivalent of learning that deep space, in all its size and darkness, was in fact an acre of Cocoa Marsh.

"I can't believe it," I said.

But Derwent quite convincingly waved his hand over the collection of porno magazines, and said, "Try."

It was as if, at the absolute center of my mind, a carefully painted still life had been tilted and real grapes rolled out of the bowl.

Derwent merely smiled.

He bent over and began shuffling the magazines back into the briefcase. When the magazines were replaced, the clasps clicked shut, and the case slid back under the bed, Derwent stood up.

"Okay, now what's your order of business?"

I was still shaken by what I'd witnessed, still agape. It seemed indecent to go directly from these photos of the sliced, glistening pink parts of women to the elevated fact of my mother, a lady who wore clothes and jewelry, played the piano with long fingers, and skillfully drove a car. For a minute I struggled, unsure what to do. Then, taking a deliberate deep breath, and in a more or less normal voice, I said, "I think my mom has a boyfriend."

Derwent, in the middle of looking for a comic book on the floor, stopped, straightened slowly up, and said, "Really?"

"Yeah, I've been keeping up surveillance operations around the house. There's a pattern of phone calls, heavy makeup, and long drives in the car—solo. My parents don't talk much anymore at home, and when they do they fight. Plus, there's this."

I withdrew a small Tupperware container from my shopping bag, pried off the top with a tiny *whoosh*, and handed him the letters I'd kept that Harta had received from the "Drexel Mental Health Clinic." Derwent studied the documents intensely for a minute, making a small humming sound under his breath.

"Got anything else?" he asked.

"Tons," I said, withdrawing a folder filled with block-printed extracts from my journals, phone logs, and surveillance notebooks. If anyone would know what to do with these materials, it would be Derwent, who was an experienced conspiracy theorist in his own right. After a minute of study he looked up at me with narrowed eyes.

"You should know we're talking actual sex here," he said.

"What do you mean?"

"You're just a kid, playing war in the backyard and intercepting your mom's mail. But what we're face-to-face with here is real sex, big time and all the way. You know those supersonic dog whistles? It's like your mom has one in her body. Guys can sense it. Their heads turn, they listen, and they make a beeline, buddy, they Get On Board. It's called natural law. Ring a bell?"

"Yeah," I lied unenthusiastically, "it rings a bell."

"The fact is," said Derwent, "your mom reeks of it."

"What?"

"Sex, Dagwood."

"My mother, are you crazy?" The thought was revolting for a second, and then suddenly it wasn't—at all.

"Okay, fine, Derwent," I said quietly, putting my hands up on either side of my head, hoping to get him to change the subject. A strange warmth was crawling across my chest. "The only reason I'm here is because I need your help in finding the guy."

Pleased with my discomfort, he fanned the materials I'd given him out on his lap, bent slightly forward, and smiled.

"I'd like to hazard a brilliant guess," he said.

"Go ahead."

"A doctor."

"A doctor what?"

"A doctor as the mysterious Mr. X. A doctor, I'm saying, is wedging your mom."

"Wedging?"

Derwent slowly stuck his index finger in and out of his mouth. I got the idea.

"How do you know?"

"All these letters from mental clinics and nuthouses. For your brother, is it?"

"Yeah."

"Anyway," said Derwent, "I'll begin on this tomorrow."

He tapped a knuckly finger on the oaktag folder. "We have to run distribution curves on the data points, and see which markers pop up. Me, an adding machine, and some math books will give us the right man. Numbers don't lie. It may take a few days, but we'll get to the bottom. Of something. In the meantime, I want surveillance intensified. Have you ever miked the shower stall? People let their guard down near running water. Look for body clues—how they sit, which way their legs are crossed. Hair has a mind of its own. Is your dad's combed away or toward her? What direction are their shoes lined up under the bed? Any parental ficky-fick? If so, how long, how hard? Does your mom scream? Mine sniffles. There's a hundred things like that. Espionage is in the details. We're talking serious. The summer's about to get *interesting*."

TWO

As I walked slowly back up the hill from Derwent's house, I was excited at the thought that all the peculiar goings-on at my home might have a simple source: a doctor! It made perfect sense, because my mother was obsessed with doctors. She kept a map of the area around our house taped to a corkboard near the TV, and had salted the map with galaxies of silver pins, each of which flew a tiny paper pennant from its top: black for doctors we still had to see, and red for doctors we already had. In another corner of the TV room lay a pile of books thick as telephone directories and filled with endless lists of state offices. On a shelf below that, hidden usually under several other books, was her private notebook, my weekly target.

It was a blue cloth binder just like one used in school, but because of what was in it, I could never see it in quite the same light as social studies. In this book Harta kept detailed records of our visits to the "health professionals," as she called the doctors. Written in tiny letters slanting backward like brushed hair were her notes on childhood autism, secondary schizophrenia with marked anxiety disorders, juvenile developmentally disabled syndrome, and those other words

12   that, when I read them, seemed literally to broadcast cold
headaches into the air above the page. Also there were the
results of tests with names like Minnesota Multiphasic, Pea-
body Picture Vocabulary, and Stanford-Binet. And there were
commands to herself that seemed to occur after certain doctors
in particular. *Chin up!* was linked to visits to Dr. Feibenbush,
while *Patience—at all costs* seemed to be her way to counter
regular visits to Dr. Stone.

Other mothers I knew coached their children in tennis or
cheerleading, driving fifty miles over bad roads for the right instructor. I saw these mothers standing with quiet pride at their
daughters' violin recitals, nodding along to the music. I
watched them instructing their sons in the identity of birds and
plants, pointing out clouds in the sky and countries on a globe.
These other mothers often had boyishly cut hair; they wore
pointy sneakers and casual skirts. They seemed to exist in a
quiet trance of understanding with their children, to be softly
nudging them forward, grooming them for a leading position in
the race of life. Our mother? Our mother went to doctors.

I opened the front door on a soaring burst of violin music from
the hi-fi, and began climbing the back staircase toward my
room. I wanted to make some notes of the conversation with
Derwent, and mark down also the approximate dates by which
we'd have a confirmed boyfriend-suspect, and following that,
a plan. But when I entered my bedroom, I saw him sitting on
my bed. His skinny shoulders were jumping. His bitten fingers
were twisting on his lap. His head was bowed and his brown
curly hair, seen from above, seemed to turn inward toward a
central point at the top of his skull like dirty water rushing
down a drain. I stood there and thought what I always thought
when I came upon my brother by surprise: This person was
almost me.

"Denny," he said tonelessly, looking straight in front of him.

"What?"

"Hit me."

"I don't think so."

"Hit me so I can do something," he repeated in his loud, dead voice.

"No, and Fad?" I said.

"What?"

"Get out of my room."

"Why," he asked, "when I touch the grass is it like eating soup in my head?"

"I don't know."

"Mommy said if I'm a good boy and a busy bee I can be happy and stay at home forever and ever. Is that good?"

"No."

"She told me the man who said that thing to me was not a nice man."

This was interesting, suddenly. I took a step closer.

"Which man was that?"

"He said something and then Mommy said something back, then he laughed."

"At you?"

"Maybe he was, maybe he just laughed. Then Mommy got angry. You know what?"

"What?"

"After that, we went away."

"Where was this?"

"In the store called Macy's, but Denny?"

"Yes?"

"We're brothers, right?"

I sighed. We'd been through this before. Idly glancing

out the window I saw a dense, upstanding cloud shaped like a dog on all fours, preparing to spring.

"What do you think, Fad?"

"That we have the same parents, right?"

I didn't answer, and as if to neatly box his own question, he picked up a piece of scrap paper and began to flick it in his fingers. He strummed the paper like an instrument and, as he did, began his noise again—his high, keening sound, which seemed to indicate the absence of problems, the presence of simple joy. As I watched, the paper became a shimmer, an arc of light green between his fingers. His face drew back hard on its bones, and after a moment, he began to scream.

I turned to the window. Mr. Mackenzie, the bald-headed crazy neighbor across the street, was mowing his driveway, gravel chiming on the blades. When I turned back, Fad was quietly inspecting his hand from an inch away, blinking rapidly.

"Guess what?" I asked.

"What?" he said to his hand.

"I heard Mommy say that we're taking you to Dr. Runsterman tomorrow."

Fad looked up at me, his eyes sharp.

"I don't like doctors," he said.

"I don't like them either, but I don't have to go to one." I leaned closer for emphasis.

"You do."

Still holding my gaze, his head began to swim back and forth on his neck. I knew what this meant: Thought in Progress.

"Okay," he said tonelessly, and then put his hand in his mouth and bit it.

I was not surprised. Fad often bit his hand when distressed. The meaty web of thumb and forefinger bore a bright red sash of scar tissue. When younger, his head sufficed. He banged it with great gusto on the floor, the walls, and a particular slice of concrete in the basement. The concussions traveled up through the beams of the house like heartbeats.

Thick, forking streams of blood were now running down his hand.

"What am I doing?" he said, taking his hand out of his mouth. He was breathing heavy.

"You're biting, Fad."

"That's right," he said. "Why?"

"I dunno."

"Good," he said, and put the hand back in his mouth. Chomping, he went over to my desk and turned on the radio. A song by the Supremes called "Where Did Our Love Go?" sprang into the room. The beat throbbed. The thick music jumped and spun. High in the air above the song, the voice of Diana Ross cried and broke perfectly, and then broke again.

"I'm bleeding," said Fad.

"Yeah, so what?"

"It's lots."

I stared and saw that blood was actually leaping into the air off his hand. I felt vaguely ill.

"Should I get Mom?"

"Sure!" he said with sudden energy, as if I'd proposed a second helping of his favorite dish. "She could bring"—he furrowed his brow, looking at his hand—"Bactine!"

When I went into the kitchen Harta was sitting in a chair staring out into the woods. I followed her gaze to the backyard where a small sprinkler was raising a claw of water, dropping it to and fro on the lawn. The lawn was faded the color of old dollar bills because over the course of the previous winter the snow and ice had drawn all the nutrients out of it, and left the grass the equivalent of breathless.

"Fad's bleeding," I said.

Harta turned to me with her gaze still fixed on the distance. Her eyes gradually focused on me, climbing up a ladder of slow eyeblinks. I realized she had been about to cry.

"He's what?" she said thickly, blowing her nose.

"Bleeding, Mom, from biting his hand."

She shook her head slowly. Then she got to her feet.

"Where?"

I raised my hand and flicked my index finger upward. She left the room and I soon heard the slow, heavy thumps of her taking the stairs.

THREE

Part of the problem, from my perspective, was that no one would have believed me. It was clear that we weren't like other families I saw around me—swift, calm, polite groupings of people like the Knoxes or the Sullivans who spoke in subdued mutterings, had perfectly parted hair, and did things like play touch football and roughhouse together—and yet to whom could I confess our strangeness? Max was indifferent, my friends would have laughed in my face, and Harta always claimed that ours was a family with only a normal dash of nuttiness—no more, no less. Whenever I disputed this, whenever I tried to explain to her that we were one of the craziest, bizarre, most twisted families that ever lived, I received the very same speech.

"Every family has a story behind it," she always began, shrugging her shoulders, as if, with that small inward motion of the bones, she might remove herself entirely from blame. "Nothing is what it seems. People walking down the street arm in arm have problems with their grandparents, honey, who are locked in their rooms upstairs and fed with snorkels. There's a thing that happens when the mother runs off with some local man, or the kids get arrested, or the parents have

18 a fistfight in traffic, or some hophead breaks into the house and kills everybody. Yes"—she drew me close—"and he does it in cold blood, too. That's human nature, you understand? Show me a family, and I'll show you a secret story of suffering, baby, and of misery and disappointment and broken dreams. See, we're just like everybody else." She was beaming. "It's a beautiful day out. Would you like some lemonade?"

I shook my head. She was wrong, I knew she was wrong, and I was determined, by hook or by crook, to prove it.

Perhaps this lay behind my obsession with espionage, an obsession I felt inside me as a voice that continually cried "Aha!" every time I peeled back the cheerful, sunny surface of life and revealed the bottomless dark within. If only my parents had sat me down, just once, and said, "You're right, you know. Our depraved obsession with keeping your crazy brother home and out of an institution is ruining this family, and causing us, more importantly, to overlook the wide variety of your own sterling qualities, especially your large and fluent vocabulary, Denny." If they had done that, I'm sure I would have simply dropped the telescopic reconnaissance from the attic window. I would have done away with the daily perimetric search of the property. The desk drawers opened, the wallets splayed and inventoried, clothing gauged for the date of its use, envelopes steamed open, the shoes observed for patterns of wear—all this would have fallen away like the deckle-edged autumn leaves that dropped from the trees each year as if eager to return to the calm, quiet world of the earth.

Instead, I not only did these things, I tabulated and alphabetized the information as well. A dresser drawer groaned with notebooks, each of which bore a title block-printed in silver Magic Marker. There was FONE FUN and TELL-THE-SCOPE. There was HOUSEHOLD HINTS and THE HOLE TRUTH. In addition, I had acquired a fingerprint kit from mail order, which enabled me to dust the bathrooms and maintain a running catalog of my parents' medical habits. Max, I learned, was predisposed toward Milk of Magnesia, which was literally stuccoed with the intricate cloverleafs of his fingerprints. Harta, for reasons of her own, tended toward Pepto-Bismol and Serutan elixir. How much simpler it all would have been if they'd simply admitted I was right, sent Fad away, and let us all relax together, espionage thrown out the window. I was a very good spy, disciplined, flexible, technologically up-to-date. But not a million sleuths working around the clock would have gotten to the bottom of what was wrong with my brother.

We left for Dr. Runsterman at eight the next morning. Fad sat next to me in the rear seat as Harta backed the throbbing car down the driveway, where it scraped a moment on the flange of the asphalt apron. The Corvair, a rare gift from Max, was very beautiful and lacquered a color called kelly green. Just standing there, it had the shape of speed to it. I thought it was dangerous and glamorous—like a movie star.

"Get your ice-cold apples!" Harta cried, as the car, pointed down the hill, began rolling fast. We passed the Donadios' house, where I had once seen a live drunken woman lying on the stoop with her skirt jacked up around her waist and her underwear showing. We passed the Wrigleys', where a fat girl who was rumored to "do things" with boys lived.

After ten minutes' driving, we threaded the coiling entrance ramp and drove with a *whoosh* onto the interstate.

"When will the road end?" asked Fad, straining forward against the acceleration.

"What, dear?" Harta rummaged in her purse for change with long fingers, getting ready for the tollbooth. I had been pleading with her to get a toll gun, which fired the chiming silver bullets of quarters into the exact change scoops—which, after a fashion, fed the highway.

"Where does it go, the road?"

"Well"—she pursed her lips—"I think it goes to Canada, actually." She laughed. "If you were crazy enough to want to go to Canada!"

"Why?" I asked.

"Brrrr!" she said, and made a tiny, inadvertent lip fart. "It's too cold for most people."

"But a lot of people live there," I said sensibly.

"And then where?" asked Fad.

"What, honey?"

"Then where does it go, in Canada?"

"I—I don't actually know, to tell you the truth."

"But Mommy." His voice was beginning to rise. "It must go somewhere. The road just can't stop. It has to get somewhere, Mommy. Mommy!"

"Yes, dear."

"Mommy find out where the road goes, make it that it goes someplace I know. Where does it go? Where?"

"The sea," I said calmly.

"What?" he turned, wild-eyed.

"Your brother's right," said Harta. "It goes where all roads go. To the ocean."

"The sea?" Fad asked, visibly relaxing.

"Yeah," I said, "they mean the same thing."

Ten minutes later, gravel from the doctor's parking lot rose against the car with a sound of weak applause. I looked up at the generic low white building in front of us. Dr. Runsterman, Harta had told her friends, was her "last hope."

But then again, according to my records, she'd already said that eight times.

We entered his office and I was left alone, as usual, in

the waiting room. Outside the windows, rain began to fall, a
tired summer rain, the dotted lines seeming to walk slowly
across the landscape, like men. Doctors' waiting rooms were
numbingly similar, one to the next: fish tank, padded chairs,
stacks of magazines, straggling plants propped on sticks, and
a large oil painting, usually of the sea, which was sometimes
shown in midstorm, busy with tall waves, high winds, and if
I was lucky, a clipper ship heeled way over to one side, its
decks already taking on water.

The rain slackened, then stopped altogether. I sat idly
perusing a *Highlights* magazine. There were diagrams where
you connected the dots and made faces appear, laughing
woodland animals, city buildings. There were spelling tests
and grammar quizzes. I remembered disdainfully when such
things had been a challenge. But that was years ago, when I
was just a kid. Now I was a highly skilled intelligence oper-
ative with perfect table manners and a flair for words.

When I looked up from my thoughts I noticed that the
receptionist had stepped away to the bathroom. It was time.
Scooting down a chilly corridor toward the familiar singsong
of her voice, I turned a corner and came upon Harta in her
usual pose, crouching forward from a chair at the center of a
dark-paneled office. Harta bent down to retrieve a dropped
piece of paper, causing her chest to be crushed flat on her
knees. Didn't that hurt? I looked at Dr. Runsterman's eyes.
They were pointed like daggers at Harta's breasts.

"Really," she was saying, "this is simply not possible,
Doctor." She acknowledged me with a tiny nod: You Can Stay.
"We've done everything you asked us to do, spent money and
time, and now you tell me that you've learned nothing, that
we're no farther down the road than we were before, and that
commission is the only recommended choice for the future.
How can that be?" Harta's voice was beginning to turn reedy,

a sign that emotions were rising in her upper chest, that she was getting ready to cry.

"Mrs. Graubart," said Dr. Runsterman, a lean, tall man with tiny glasses and a jaw like a bicycle seat, "the castle of psychology has many a winding stair, to misquote a line of schoolboy poetry. We're not dealing with microbes here, but with the human mind. Forget penicillin and the silver bullet. We're still deep in the dark in many ways." The doctor leaned backward in his chair with a squeak, raised one hand, and pinched his forefinger and thumb together in an illustration of "in the dark." He was wearing a white smock like a barber's, and you could see the faint blackness of his underarm hair through the fabric. "James, I've already told you, falls into a diagnostic gray zone. The etiology of his disorder is mystifying, to put it mildly."

I glanced at the subject of their conversation. He was standing behind the doctor and Harta, staring out a window at the rainy scene. His arms were extended straight in the air on either side of his body, and, just perceptibly, he was tilting forward and back. I realized after a moment that he was imitating, with the shape of his body, the giant crucifix atop the church across the street. He opened his mouth, stuck out his tongue. After a while, watching, I stuck my tongue out, too.

"I think that at a certain point we have to employ a comprehensive approach to problem solving," the doctor was saying.

"What do you mean by that?" Harta asked, leaning back in her chair.

"I mean that the entire overall health of the family has to be considered," said the doctor. "I mean," he said, raising a yellow pencil and pointing it toward where I stood with my tongue out, tasting the dry indoor air, "for example, the health of your other son."

As we left, minutes later, Harta spoke to the doctor and nurses in her special politely chilly way, as if tasting a chain of individually sour words, that meant only one thing: Once again, a doctor had let her down, and once again, she would refuse to accept his verdict. For six months straight I had been monitoring phone calls from doctors with savory names like Finkelkraut, Leiberstein, and Schwartzman, recording these conversations on my Webcor reel-to-reel through a patch attached to the pink basement Princess. The tapes were stored in a shoebox marked *Good Stuff*, and consisted for the most part, of professionally crisp voices telling my mother that Fad was in their opinion seriously disturbed, and that it was wrong, deeply injurious to the health of her family, to keep him at home.

And yet, no matter the seriousness and force of these various doctors—on phones increasingly, but also in high-altitude offices, in lobbies, and in the dead white light of examining rooms—Harta refused to budge an inch. Fad would stay at home locked within the charmed circle of her arms, attending specialized day schools, and this, she made it clear, was nonnegotiable. Never, if she could help it, would he be sent to a "mental institution," with, as I imagined it, a name like Greymoor, an electrified fence, and a staff of men dressed in bloody smocks who would slowly suck out his brain with basting syringes.

When Fad dragged the heel of his shoe down my shin so that long upstanding petals of flesh peeled off and I bled for days; dropped a phone on my head while I slept and filled my new shoes with mud; when I was out at the movies one day and he shit in my bed, he was "just expressing his love, reversed," Harta explained. She said this as she disinfected the bite marks on my forearms, put a compress on the swelling egg on my forehead, or iced my stomped foot, and she added that Fad was "dealing as well as can be expected with the frustrations of someone in his situation, sweetie." In her mind, he simply deserved to be protected, like certain kinds of butterflies or vanishing species of birds. She would do this for the very simple reason that she loved him. She loved him eternally. She loved him as the earth, it was somehow implied to me, loved the moon for making tides.

FOUR

I didn't know why Max drank so much, but I guessed it had something to do with all that. My surveillance notebooks were increasingly filling with observations like *Suspect A, showing instability on his feet near the piano* or *Wobbling of Main Man caused a glass to slip through his fingers to the floor, and go* smash! As baseball season heated up and Mickey Mantle began once again slamming balls high into the air over Yankee Stadium, my interest was evenly split between the tiny diving figures on the television set and that other spectacle: Max's drinking. It was clear that over the last few months—since January, and the beginning of Harta's strange behavior—his drinking had only deepened and intensified. According to what I'd overheard Harta telling friends on the phone, Max was drinking hard at lunch each day. And every night upon returning home from work, he now headed straight for the rack of bottles with beautiful labels on them like old documents, and swung one high into the air. The precious liquid bubbled a moment at his mouth, and then it happened: His face bulged. His eyes watered. He wiped his hands across his lips, looked around like someone awakened from a long deep sleep, and suddenly he was better. Sometimes he tweaked my ear, and wanted abruptly to talk about boxing or the miracle of magnetism. Other times his eyes sparkled a moment, his face drew up on one side, and then he fell, suddenly, asleep.

Curious, I had once tried drinking liquor from the bottles in Max's cabinet. Scotch, when I sipped it, burned like a string of tangled fire in my throat. Vodka bristled with the chill of outer space. And yet these liquids worked on Max like the muriatic acid he poured on calcium deposits in the bathroom sink, melting away the salts of hardness in his face, turning his voice mellow with reminiscence.

But not always.

On June 17, Roger Maris, in a rare return to form, whacked a tremendous game-winning home run over the left-field wall of Yankee Stadium with a sound like a gunshot, and though I felt the entire insides of my body rising to meet the ball as it rushed away into the sky, I turned off the set, jumped to my feet, and ran halfway down the stairs. Max was parking the car with a certain telltale thrashing sound of the transmission, and I wanted to confirm my hunch. Through the wrought-iron curlicues of the banister, I watched him open the door and stand swaying and muttering to himself in the hallway. Sure enough, as we sat down to dinner ten minutes later, it was clear he was quite drunk—perhaps, in his own words, even "boiled."

Because it was a weeknight, we ate that evening in the kitchen. But then again, we were always in the kitchen. The kitchen was the neural center of the house, switching station for a thousand impulses a day. Sitting in the ladderback chair, I studied Max's face unhappily for a moment, and then dropped my eyes to the doctored bowl of Cream o' Vegetable soup in front of me. Harta had loaded "extra nutrients" into the gummy liquid, code for broccoli and cabbage, each of which I found disgusting.

I smiled hatefully in the breeze of vegetable odors.

"Mommy," said Fad, stirring his soup with a fork.

"Yes?" She turned with the main course bubbling in a casserole dish, and leaned forward through the mist in a way that gave her the look of an apparition, like Casper.

"Will you play something on the piano after dinner?" he asked.

"Of course I will, honey."

"What are you going to play?" I asked, poking a dead adult celery stalk.

Harta put her hands on her hips and smiled. "Since when have you ever cared what I played?"

"I don't know," I said, which was true.

Max said nothing at all, weirdly.

"Stravinsky!" cried Fad, and gave me a gloating look.

Max seemed to grow more tired.

"Poppy?" Harta sat down at the table. "Is everything okay at work?"

He looked at her levelly.

"Work's fine," he said.

"What does?" asked Fad. "Not me. I don't work fine. I don't work at all do I Daddy?"

"Stop," said Harta. "Leave your father alone for now."

"Why?" I asked, sensing an opening.

"Because he's tired."

A small, heat-seeking probe would do. "He's always tired," I said calmly.

Max's face rode up on one side, and he leaned forward toward me across the table. "Okay, now listen you little ba—"

"Who's for juice?" Harta cried in a loud voice, jumping to her feet.

There was a pause, just long enough to take a breath. I did.

"Not me," said Max slowly, sighing and settling back down in his chair. "But I'll have a beer."

"Another?" asked Harta, making a hissing sound.

I cleared my throat, or rather swallowed. Light, pulsing from an overhead fluorescent ring fixture, fell down on us again and again. I decided to launch my theme.

"Being normal," I stated, "is important." No one said anything. "It's important," I went on, "because it allows you to do things in life, like staying at home and raising children who are happy and mentally healthy."

Harta shot me a look. But Fad, if he understood what I said, only seemed to enjoy it. He placed his long, bitten hands between his knees and pressed hard, while his lips pulled back like on the squashed faces of men riding centrifuges such as I'd seen once in *Life* magazine. Meanwhile, from his mouth there came a tiny sibilant whistling sound. It was Fad's version of crowing. But was he overjoyed at my normal-talk? That seemed strange.

Max poured the beer, and as it foamed up, cut his eyes to Fad. "No wheeing at the table," he said, but almost gently.

"Wheeing" we called it.

"Daddy," said Fad.

"Being normal is important," I repeated, though with considerably less volume.

"Oh yeah?" said Harta. "Why?"

"What, son?" asked Max.

"Mainly," I said, "because it allows people to have happy families without worrying about the State."

Harta turned from the stove, lips jerking angrily on her face, but Fad broke in before she had a chance to speak.

"Daddy?" he asked calmly. "When I put my finger in my ass, why is it like a plane taking off?"

Staring at the colorful slew of food on my plate, I felt the entire air of the room seize up, begin to chill.

I glanced at Max, who had templed his hands over his nose, giving his eyes the staring disembodied look of those on the back of the dollar bill.

"I have told you," he said with dangerous slowness, his words falling like stones through the air, "that I will not tolerate vulgarity at the dinner table."

And then, just then, at that very moment, to my great disappointment, the doorbell rang. I slumped in my chair as Harta, with a long, relieved sigh, said, "Ah, that must be him now."

"Who?" I asked.

"The man from the state mental health agency, Mr. George," she said, looking at me significantly, and touching her neck below the ear. I followed the pointer of her finger out to her face and noticed she was wearing lots of makeup and that her hair was piled on her head. Her lips seemed redder than normal, a bright, arterial color.

"What kind of a last name is that, 'George'?" I asked. "Is it, like, a mistake his parents made?"

"Dunno," said Max, seeming to wake up all of a sudden, "but I'll tell you this." He finished the remains of his beer in a gulp and cracked open another with a tiny flaring hiss. I leaned close, hoping to get in on the secret he was about to divulge. "The only mistake *we* ever made was named Denny Graubart."

I was used to these cruel random slashes from Max when

drunk. Harta, on the way out of the room, turned and frowned as Max laughed loudly.

"Don't start, please," she said.

"Did somebody tell a joke?" asked Fad in his off-kilter voice.

"I'm just getting warmed up," said Max. "And now"—he turned to Harta and waved the beer in an extravagant gesture, yellow liquid rushing the top of the bottle; some of it dribbled between his fingers—"I think it incumbent upon you as chatelaine to escort our a-steamed guest into the living room."

"What does that mean, what you just said?" I asked. No one answered. Harta left and a moment later I heard the front door open and then a murmur of voices. I was getting ready to leave the table and investigate when Max, sighting at me over the foamy top of his Schlitz, said, "Pow, you're dead! And now that you are, stay just where you are, chief. Don't move." Leaning forward, he whispered, "We need to let her soften him up."

"Okay," I whispered back, having no idea what he was talking about.

Satisfied, Max drank his beer, his Adam's apple bobbing as he swallowed. When the beer was about halfway done, he turned toward me and belched quietly.

"Ah, the lost art of conversation," he said with a sigh. "Get ready, son. We're about to have a chat."

"Really?" I said.

Max finished his beer in a series of noisy swallows. "Yup," he said. "I don't like this any more than you do, but here goes." He wiped his mouth with the back of his hand. "Denny, your mother is worried about you. She thinks you're spending too much time up in your room alone—says you're becoming increasingly 'withdrawn.' " Max pronounced the word with faint distaste. "Wants me to ask you if anything's 'bothering' you. You look A-one to me, you little pirate. But just so your mom doesn't squawk too loud, I'll ask you: Is there anything you want to talk about?"

I looked at him a moment. He was staring into the air directly over my head, his face with its familiar knobs and folds opened just then in a vacant smile. With all my heart I wanted to shout, Yes, Dad, let's talk about us, why don't we. Stoop down from your remote cloud-mountain and speak to *me*, for once. Touch me, Max. Show me the secret science of the curve in a thrown baseball, explain the origins of oceans to me, and why it is Saturn perches like a derby in deep space. As I watched, he poured himself another beer, knocked it back with an oddly delicate gesture, and then leveled a stare at me. His eyes, I noticed, were rather bloodshot.

"Nah," I said.

"Right," muttered Max, as if in confirmation of some long-standing hunch. A moment later Harta returned from the front door, leaned back into the kitchen, and jerked her eyes toward the living room.

"Drink?" asked Max. "Does he want?" He made pantomime gestures with one hand.

She shook her head coldly. "No, that's your department. Just come meet the man."

"A husband's work is never done," said Max, heaving himself to his feet with a sigh. He looked at Fad and me. "Don't grow up," he said. "Stay a kid." He threw a high, looping mock punch at my jaw. "It's cheaper."

He began to leave the room, but stopped and turned. In the interim, he had composed his features, sharpened the blur on his face to focus. He spoke crisply. It was as if his drunkenness were operated by a string in his pocket he could pull or loosen at will.

"Take your brother upstairs," he said quickly. "Don't worry about dinner, we can finish it later. Just do it. *Now.* And up the back staircase. I want things very quiet around here for the next hour."

When they left I sat at the table a moment, uncertain what to do. Clearly, I had been excluded. Once again I had been barred from the throbbing, busy center of the house. It was the world they were trying to keep me out of, the world of busy people streaming down the streets and rising and falling in the peristalsis of elevators. What was I left with? A soft "Sha," from Harta. A "Don't you dare!" from Max. A brother looking at me from across the dinner table now with a smile on his face like a cracked plate. He was rocking slowly forward and back. And then it came to me.

"Geed," I said. It was our password extraordinaire, coded entrance to our private world.

Fad looked at me, his eyes flashing with pleasure.

"Califundulay," he whispered, topping me.

I paused, challenged. "Yumickuleh," I came back with. Fad, overjoyed, placed his hands between his legs, squeezed his knees. His mouth was working, the entire mask of his face lifted a moment in his jammed-ecstatic look.

"Fantoopenstein!" he trumped.

I giggled. From the living room I could hear the pleasant three-way hum of voices engaged in conversation. I smiled to myself, nodding along to the conversation, waiting for a lull. Harta was saying something insistently, her voice rising as if to make a point, then sinking back down on itself. I knew that liquid seesaw sound. It meant she wanted something, was trying to get something. But what? There was a sudden silence. It was time.

"Fuckenberg!" I whispered.

Fad's ecstatic look dropped. His face grew serious and

accusing. And then, to my delight, his eyes filled as I knew they would and he began to cry.

"Mommy!" he screamed. "He said a bad word! Denny, he made a filthy one!"

The voices ceased. A moment later Harta, then Max, appeared at the door.

"He's usually so calm," said Harta, bestowing a brilliant smile on Mr. George, a balding, roly-poly man whose face had just been poked into the room and was now coming rapidly into focus in astonishment.

"Honey? Darling?" she said desperately to Fad, who if he heard her gave no sign at all. He was just then far too involved in studying the enormous wound that my dirty word had opened up in his mind.

With great dignity I said, "I only asked him if he wanted a fork."

But Fad sobbed and wailed and carried on, crying like I'd broken his heart.

My brother was eventually quieted, and Mr. George ushered out into the night. But the experience had left something ringing in my head, and later that night, I found myself unable to sleep. Tossing on my hot pillow, I heard voices erupt from Max and Harta's bedroom, and, curious, I sidled out of my room and into the hallway. On a flowing wave of air the words arrived bell-clear.

"It was a setback, all right, but I do have a new plan," Harta was saying.

Max didn't say anything for a long while, then said, "Yeah?"

"Yes, it's a special new kind of home training, and if I have your full support, we may be able to keep him out of that awful place."

"Which place?"

"Take your pick, Max. They're all equally terrible."

"Honey, let's try to be realistic."

"Realistic—about what?"

"That little thing called the future? I don't want to rain on anyone's parade, least of all yours, but I gotta say, the signs aren't exactly, uh, encouraging. You have a boat that's beginning to sink, you bail it, right? But if the boat's not seaworthy, well, my father always taught me that at a certain point you have to—"

"What the hell are you talking about? A boat, did you say? A *boat*? Sometimes, Max, I've gotta say, you amaze even me. To think that—hey, what are you doing?"

"Nothing, dear. Just getting comfortable."

"It used to be called getting pregnant. Leave me alone."

"You're funny. A funny funny girl, always were and always will be. Remember those evenings on Lake George?"

"Yes, I remember Lake George. I also remembered it the last time you asked me, a week ago."

"Be nice, Harta."

"Be sober, Max. It's ruining your memory."

I heard what I took to be Max falling back in bed. But what had he been doing, standing?

"Ah, just forget it," said Max.

"With pleasure, darling."

"Harta?"

"I *said* I'd forgotten it. Now let me sleep."

"Can we talk?"

There was a pause. Then Harta sighed. "Okay," she said, "if you want to 'talk' so badly all of a sudden, let's talk about this."

"What is it?"

Papers rustled. I was now up against the door, my ear

pressed to the cool wood. I had never done this before, judging it too risky. But the strange, spiraling conversation had gradually drawn me in.

"The brochure for Ramphill Village. Take a look. If the home training doesn't work this summer, I'm beginning to think it's where we're going to end up."

"Looks pretty impressive, actually. Nice grounds."

"We may take a trip up there next month. Want to come?"

"I'd love to, honey, but that's July, remember? Time for the annual inventory—Marvin is on my ass, and Mr. Macnamara—"

"That's enough, please. I was joking anyway."

"What about?"

"Asking you to come."

"Why?"

"Why? Because I know you is why. And by the way, do you call this a talk?"

"Maybe just a little well-meaning chat?"

There was the click of a light going off.

"Not even that," said Harta.

FIVE

After many days of building density in the air, a heat wave exploded in the last week of June. I had once burned spiders with a magnifying glass—the cone of concentrated sunlight bearing down on the living creature, which flared up suddenly in a writhing wisp of smoke. As the heat wave took hold, the same burning cone now felt suspended gigantically in the air above our house. By three o'clock every afternoon the roads had grown soft and sticky to the touch, and in the evening, a kind of heat-mist, like breath, gathered in the spaces beneath the trees. I kept myself occupied by reading desert survival manuals while listening to the attic fan paddle the heavy air, or watched the giant thermometers on television weather reports rising into the blood-colored danger zones while "meteorologists" stood next to them, whisking pointers to and fro and warning people they'd be risking their lives if they went outside in "the freak tropical conditions." During those days the deep, refreshing fact of cold seemed gone forever, removed from our lives. And though the television said one afternoon that an American named Jim Ryun had run the mile in the astonishing time of three minutes and fifty-one seconds, I knew he couldn't possibly have done it in anything like the tent of broiling air lying over our backyard.

On the fifth day of the heat wave the letter arrived. I was up in the attic that afternoon, rowing the skinny green telescope back and forth over the terrain that dropped away from our house down the hill, when I saw the mailman turn the corner onto the bottom of our street and begin the long, laborious climb up.

"No!" cried Fad, somewhere below my feet.

A scattering of dusty instruments was arrayed around me in the attic: sextants, theodolites, backstaffs, and heliographs, things with long darkwood fingers and tiny knobs and mirrors attached.

"Okay!" screamed Fad.

They were relics of Max's dead passion for navigation, instruments for measuring distance and location that optically racked the planets like pool balls and strung invisible lines, sun to moon, star to star. "Space," Max had once assured me, "looks still to us, but it's boiling like a pot of water for tea. The earth? A single drop, a pinprick of wetness. What do you think that makes you, big shot?"

The mailman seemed to float in a flag of waving heat lines. I focused in hard on his figure crouching in a doorway halfway up the hill. Strange mirrory strands flashed in the atmosphere—as if, I thought, under pressure of the blazing summer heat the air itself was changing, the fan belts of molecules beginning to droop, the whirring electric dance of life to slow.

A long hand floated out the door toward the mailman in a beautiful movie gesture, followed by a swirl of pink dress, like a glass of champagne. A rush of blond hair fell into the light a moment, then swung back inside the house. After a second, the arm flowed out again, this time bearing a glass of something the mailman drank deeply of. He drew one leg up, leaning as he swallowed.

I watched carefully as the mailman finished his drink, handed it back with a flourish, and made a gallant little bow of departure. He was just turning to go when the arm, drifting again out the door, hooked him around the neck, and drew him stumbling into the house.

At last! Frantically, I consulted my chart of the neighborhood: the house he had been dragged into belonged to the Claridge family—father, Ross, an electronics engineer; mother, Cynthia; and one teenage son, Alexander, vaguely associated with a gang of petty larcenists called the Cahoots.

"I'll have six!" cried Fad.

At high speed I wrote in my log: *Letter carrier coerced into home. Code Three in effect. Take all necessary measures.* Reaching for the phone, I dialed the post office with nervous fingers. A sleepy voice answered, "Post office, Jacobson."

"Officer," I blurted, "I want to report a crime."

"Really, son?" The voice sounded amused. "I'm not a policeman, you know. I'm just a clerk." He pronounced it Clark, as in Kent.

I tried to make my voice deeper, more powerful, but it dwindled helplessly upward.

"I think a mailman was kidnapped," I bleated.

"Kidnapped!" I heard the springs of a chair screech.

In my best *Dragnet* voice, calm but terse like Sergeant Joe Friday, I said, "I live on Forty-four Drainer Drive and I just saw a letter carrier forced into number thirty-one, the house of Mrs. Claridge."

"Hang on." There was a long pause, during which the clerk covered the phone with his hand, and I heard odd clammy piping sounds, interrupted by several hoots. When he

got back on the line, his voice was changed somehow, mel-
lower, even happy.

"Okay, son," he said, "now I want you to know that I'm
really delighted you called and am passing your information
onto the FBI. As it turns out, we have an agent standing by
for postman kidnappings of just this type, and he's ready to
get to work." There was a loud shriek of laughter in the background. "Son," said the clerk, "I'm gonna deputize you over
the phone, all right? What you have to remember first, see, is
that everything pertaining to this is absolutely classified information. You can't reveal it, and you can't talk about it. Even
to your mom and dad. Do I have your word on it?"

I could feel it: Once again, familiarly, I was being played
for a fool. Softly I replaced the phone on "Son? Son?" and
stood a moment in the attic.

"Okay!" screamed Fad, distantly.

I went and stared out the attic window for a moment,
briefly calculating the potential for fatal injury if I fell. The
comfort this sometimes brought was absent, today, for the feeling went on in my head as strong as ever that I was, after all,
a prize moron. Several long minutes went by, consumed with
energetic self-hatred. When I reapplied my eye to the telescope, I saw the mailman standing back on the front stoop of
Mrs. Claridge's, adjusting his tie. He was drawing himself up,
and staring out at the neighborhood like he might, under certain circumstances, just be convinced to buy it.

Soon he was placing the mail in the house directly
across the street, and soon after turning to approach our house.
But before he could even get to our lawn, the front door was
flung open, and Harta barreled out into the street.

She greeted him with a warm "Hi there!" and plucked
the extended letter from his hand. Then, spinning on one heel

in a way I thought distinctly weird, she trailed one arm in the air and skipped back to the house.

I had never seen her go out to retrieve the mail like that.

A muttering became audible—a familiar muttering. Fad. I panned the scope to and fro until I intercepted a blur of ambling brown moving toward the drainage ditch bordering our house. After a moment, the blur sprawled comfortably in the narrow channel. I focused on the family brow and nose, the slitted, vaguely Asiatic eyes. Fad, I noticed, was staring shyly into the sun, as if he and the fiery planet were being introduced at a formal dinner. "You," he stated in his loud, level voice, "are the mailman."

Halfway across the street, the mailman stopped, turned, mopped his brow, and said, "Sure am, that's right."

"Where does the mail come from?" asked Fad, and before the mailman could answer, swerved his head back and addressed his extended index finger, whispering to it in a loud voice, "The mail, it comes from somewhere, but where?"

Intensely still, watching, the mailman scratched his head.

"Everywhere!" cried Fad, and bent a blade of grass in his hand and began flicking it fast, his face riding up on the runners of its bones.

Colors rushed in a blur. I swung the scope away from this fallen world and back to the sky, where I escorted several tiny airliners through clouds, and watched a file of trees on a mountainside thrashing in a sudden puff of wind. An hour later, spiraling down through the house to go outside and play, I noticed that the trash bag in the kitchen sported a fresh snowfall of torn white paper bits. There was no one around in the kitchen at the moment, so, thinking fast, I scooped up the fragments and placed them in my pocket. I then took a sheet

of paper towel from the dispenser, tore it in pieces, laid these
on top of the remaining trash, and scooted up the stairs.

Back in my room, I withdrew the treasured bits of letter
and spread them carefully out on the bed, taping together
different bits and pieces. There were little bits of typed sense
that began only very slowly to have a larger coherence. I dis-
carded words, stray punctuation, an occasional entire phrase
in my attempt to find the string, the vein of sense that ran, I
was certain, through the center of the letter.

After an hour's work, I noted in one of my notebooks
the result:

Dear Harta:

If you that are there would come by advisory,
our weekly conditioning might operant better than
love.

H.

I grinned. I was very proud of myself. I had cracked the
code of Harta's privacy, and the summer still had nine weeks
to go.

That night, just before going to bed, I went to find Max in his
study, my mind made up to tell him about my new discovery.
When I opened the door I saw that Max, as usual, was en-
grossed in a science book—a thick dense volume with tiny
type and diagrams on its pages like swatted insects. By day
he worked as an executive at Stark Products, a plastics fac-
tory, but by night, when not in his workshop, he spent his time
in his study immersed in the history of science, which he had
once explained to me was a succession "of lonely men, in
little rooms." I stood in the doorway observing how the cone

of light over his head picked out the sharp features, the forking vein on the forehead, the full lips. As I walked in, Max looked up to greet me and I knew right away he was drunk. Where his eyes were usually sharp there was a kind of mud. His face hung fallen on its bones, abnormally slack. As I watched, the face twitched itself into an unfriendly smile.

"Hark, the Great White Hunter. How come I never see you doing homework, sonny boy?"

"There is no homework, Dad, it's the summer."

"A comedian I've got, a regular comedian for a son. You think I didn't know that?"

"Daddy?"

"Yes."

"I, uh, wanted to ask you something."

"Really?" Silently, his far hand reached down below the chair. I didn't even have to guess why. The bottle rose. The whiskey fell. It didn't matter. I cleared my throat. I was planning on saying something about how he was a good dad and he could always rely on me for help. I was then going to produce the taped-together letter from Mr. H., and ask if that was the reason he seemed so quiet and unhappy with Harta lately. If his answer was yes, then I was going to propose that we band together and do something about Mr. H., man to man— hunt him down, corner him, and shoot him like a dog, perhaps. I opened my mouth to speak, but felt suddenly a wave of enormous instability roll through me. I looked down: legs, knees, feet as usual.

"Dad, isn't it hot out?" I heard myself say.

He laughed, relieved. "As blazes, big spender. We might as well be in Rio-by-the-Sea-O!"

I laughed, too. It was so easy to be a man with Max, and have man-thoughts and share man-chuckles.

"Do you and Mommy love each other?"

Max's smile froze.

"Do we love each other?" He coughed loudly. "Do you mean do we love each other? Is that what you mean?"

"Yeah, I guess."

There was a long pause during which Max, ignoring me entirely, drank smoothly, fluently. More than ever, it was clear that what he did with the bottle was carry on a conversation, a very special, very expensive kind of conversation. Fortified by whiskey, seeming newly happy, he smacked his lips.

"Of course we do, son. Whatever gave you the impression otherwise? Your mother and I are married—remember? We've also produced two fine sons, one a famous young trial attorney."

"Ha, Dad."

"That's it, son, don't hold back. Laugh till it hurts. God, I've raised a dry one. Smile a little." Max lifted the bottle, drank, set it down. "You'll live longer."

I raised a small, lopsided grin onto my face.

"What are you poking around in all this stuff with your mom and me for, anyway?" Max asked.

"I don't know, Dad."

"You worried about something?" Max raised the book up until only his eyes were visible. They looked nervous, I thought suddenly.

"Something particular eating at ya?" he asked from behind the book.

"No."

"Figured as much." The book was lowered slightly. "Okay, if you're done wringing this witness out, we'll adjourn for the day. That all right by you, Counsel?"

"Sure."

SIX

If it wasn't the mailman arriving with an earth-shattering letter, then the tree surgeon appeared in our backyard wearing a delicate white smock. If not the plumber come to stop knocking pipes, then the Fuller Brush man rang the bell, and while standing in our doorway opened a leather case hinged like the jaws of a precious animal. Sometimes it was the delivery boy from the Du-Rite pharmacy with Fad's latest prescription. Mostly, however, it was those other people who came nearly every day at three that summer, those fragrant, well-meaning, unbearable people: Harta's friends.

Evidently an endless supply of women existed whose joy in life, as I came to understand it, was to sit in our living room, eat sponge cake, sing, play the piano, and talk in the voices of wounded animals about their husbands, themselves, and especially their children. Their mouths were heavily lipsticked, faces powdered to a crepe finish, and their hair swept into the volumetric pinnacles and arches of old buildings. Of all of them, none was louder, stranger to me, more frightening, than Harta's "dearest friend" Maude, a woman with candelabra-sized hands dipped in glittery nail polish, who had been around our family so long that her presence was something in the line of a recurring natural event, like summer rain—or hail.

"Ahhh," breathed Maude, day after day of that summer, sweeping into the living room without ringing the bell, and catching me, as often as not, by surprise. "Ehhh," she cooed, drawing near, "if I were fifteen years younger and you a little older, we'd paint the town red, wouldn't we, lover?" Clumsily, she chucked me under the chin, an inch from my windpipe. I jerked my head back and, smiling widely, decided, for the moment anyway, to refrain from hurting her unforgettably. Life already had. She had no children of her own, and this, it had been explained to me, was a kind of death sentence. "A curse," Harta had said. "A woman like her, so vibrant and alive."

"It's a blessing," Max had replied, looking up from his reading: Zygeuner's *History of Trigonometry*. "What, she should pass that clothes sense on to another human being?"

Attired in loud pantsuits and giant auroral blue streaks of eye shadow, Maude seated herself amidst the assembled bric-a-brac of our living room, pursed her lips, and with a touch of hand to back of head, began gossiping ecstatically. I witnessed these conversations from my surveillance emplacement on the second-floor-hallway carpet. For hours I lay prone, notebook in hand, while the air rose against my face, scented with the adult, metropolitan odor of Maude's perfume: My Sin.

"And so, honey?" she asked one afternoon. Her blond hair was styled in a flaming nose cone. "What's the latest at earthquake central? Is he going to make it at home?"

Harta sighed a long sigh. "James? Who can tell, Maudie. But I've decided the time"—she took a breath—"has come to try something different."

"Yes? Christ, what haven't you tried?" I watched, so

mesmerized by the light clustering around the yellow dome of Maude's hair that I didn't hear what Harta said.

"—new school of thought," I caught, when my attention returned with a little flash. "Behaviorism, it's called. A scientist worked out the whole theory with pigeons. He says that we're just machines anyway, and that all of this psychoanalysis"—Harta doodled a disparaging shape in the air with a finger—"is a bunch of self-indulgent crap."

"I couldn't agree more," said Maude smugly. "Freud ought to have his head examined."

"Right," said Harta, nodding approvingly, "and that's just what this guy, Skinnerd, out at some university, believes. He says not to get all caught up in finding the root causes of things and instead spend your time curbing the problem behaviors themselves. I've gotten a book about it, and they explain the ground rules. I'm going to begin giving James his lessons later this week. We're very excited."

She leaned forward, and in a low voice explained, "They say it's all about rewards and punishments."

"Ah," said Maude delicately, "punishment."

Maude pressed her fingertips together below her chin and then widened them rapidly outward in a kind of breast-stroke.

"Just so you know," she said, "I've been dumped."

"By who? Not the—the—" Harta fluffed her hands in the air by her head.

"Yeah, him: the Hair. Did you know he had his eyebrows plucked?"

"I never liked him," Harta said decisively. "To me I'll tell you what he was: a perfumed sharpie."

"English Leather. But he was *my* sharpie. Now what?"

Harta refilled her coffee with a long, bristling dark rope of liquid. "Doll, we each have our cross to bear," she said in her "philosophical" tone of voice. She gestured around the living room. "What do you call this? Shangri-la?"

When Maude left, I went back to my notebooks and ran a check. According to my calculations, behavioral home therapy was either the twentieth or twenty-first—my count was uncertain—in the series of handmade cures Harta had worked up for Fad. Each had been announced with a small flourish by Harta, and nearly all of them had first arrived via the mail. Every afternoon a jerky, geometric stream of pamphlets, handbills, and endless specialized correspondence addressed to Harta spewed forth from the mail slot—all of it, when possible, steamed open, perused, and resealed by me. The astonishing volume of my mother's mail functioned very much as did her visits to the doctors. After all, if people from all over the world were writing to her with claimed knowledge of how to make Fad better, how could she in good conscience possibly give up the ghost?

High Protein Leaf Meal, Vegetarian Dead Sea Extract, megavitamin injections, Magic Mud. There was one pamphlet I saw that had a four-color diagram of the brain, with a small wedge marked ANXIETY removed. Attached to this, weirdly, was a sheet of mimeograph paper describing the relationship between eyesight and psychological functioning. Another pamphlet consisted solely of a list:

1. The child who is excessively anxious without reason
2. The child who has no awareness of his own identity
3. The child who twirls
4. The child who rocks
5. The child who walks on tiptoes

6. The child who remains rigid indefinitely
7. The child who doesn't speak properly for his
   own age
8. The child who doesn't speak at all

Below this, there was no text, only an address, in San Francisco.

There was literature on massage, on aromatherapy, reflexology, and the principles of psychoanalysis. One pamphlet contained a series of photos of a special steel bar from which the brain-damaged child was to hang for an hour each day, so that "like city workers repairing a potholed street, nutrient-rich blood might gently fill in the gaps in organic functioning."

Day in, day out, the mail arrived, replete with the tiny barred windows of stamps, through which, pressing my eye close, I might gaze upon spired churches, jungles teeming with eland and gazelle, and once, in a letter from Spain, an ancient city square where men stood talking in plumed hats and waxed dagger mustaches. When the letters were too large to fit in the mail slot, they were left outside. This added an element of mystery to the mix, as they were normally Fad's test scores, or results of Harta's response to a questionnaire of some sort. Notable among the bulky arrivals was a thick manila envelope that came bearing the New Jersey state seal, a symbol composed of what appeared to be two bored knights carrying a side of beef. Inside, intriguingly, was a thick sheaf of mimeographed papers attached with a brass clasp. Typed across the top were the words JAMES GRAUBART—VISUAL-PERCEPTUAL-MOTOR INTEGRATION AND MOVIGENICS ACTIVITIES, followed by a bewildering array of columns, categories, and evaluations. Next to the word *trampolet* was written, "Jumping with total action system and visual system combined in dynamic balance and movement. Locating the central

visual target and maintaining visual contact with the surround
(figure-ground relationships and location of self while moving
and looking in space)." On the next page was the category
"Tunnel of Fun," with, written next to it, "Crawling and creeping in a crossed-pattern to provide for enhanced neurological
organization and reciprocal interweaving of two body halves
and putting two eyes together to lead to more efficient bin-
ocular vision when in an erect locomoting position." This led
to a long pleasant daydream in which I imagined Fad on all
fours puffing smoke from his mouth as he locomoted merrily
down the street, lifted one leg, and farted blue exhaust gas.

At the end of the report, on the last page, was a summary
that for some reason terrified me: "All human beings can become more efficient and function better with this training, to
meet the symbolic demands of our culture with greater success
and dignity."

I decided that the person who wrote this was someone
who, for reasons I couldn't explain exactly, was someone I
never wanted to meet.

SEVEN

The Yankees were in a slump. They had, once, years earlier, won five pennants in a row and had opened this season with the huge stadium freshly painted in the team colors of white and blue, but it was clear they were faltering. The batters couldn't bat, and the pitchers, no matter how speedily they windmilled their arms, couldn't stop getting hit. Line drives that would formerly have been snagged in a diving catch now blasted routinely through to the monuments. Also, the players seemed to run more slowly than they should have, and stared at the ground a lot as the team drifted to third, fourth, and then finally fifth place in the league. Were my beloved Yankees turning into a bunch of spazzes? I studied the papers daily in an attempt to determine what was wrong. Opinion raged. Some placed the blame entirely on the manager, Ralph Houk. Others hinted quietly that there were problems with the aging southpaw, Whitey Ford. Whatever the reason, attendance was falling, and the stands were sometimes half-filled. The flags drooped in the heat as if they knew something. Even Phil Rizzuto sometimes ran out of things to say, and spent more time than usual clearing his throat.

One afternoon I was watching a game in which the Yan-

kees were taking what the announcers called "a drubbing"
from the Boston Red Sox, when I suddenly realized that the
sounds I was hearing were not those only of the crack of the
bat and the roar of the crowd, but different sounds—entirely
new sounds. Leaning forward, I turned down the volume. Then
I stood up and walked to the very center of the room to hear
better. I couldn't believe my luck. Fad and Harta were at their
very first home lesson a room away, and I crouched there and
began listening hard.

Immediately I noticed her voice, breaking constantly
upward with a heavy, sighing, surflike motion. I imagined vowels, fanning out like ants to tug Fad's tie straight, comb his
hair, cause his cheeks to shine, his mouth to enunciate the
words in crisp, polite shapings of the lips. He would be a
public man, poised and natty. She would make him over in
the ideal image she had of our own father. And so he would
wear a tie, learn to shave, part his hair on the side. And eventually he would take over a small job—nothing too taxing. He
would grow into life diagnosed "delicate," and marry into a
family that was full of caring, slightly plump women, with a
light of niceness on their faces.

I knew she thought this. In her private moments, turning
away from the dishes into pure sunlight, or listening to music
with her mind adrift, she thought this. I knew she did.

Still listening, fascinated, I walked down the hall and
into the room. Fad sat rigid in a chair, his skeletal body curv-
ing forward like a pen stroke, reddish hair exploded off his
head, his hands in his lap making tiny pretzeled flowers of
his fingers. Harta paced to and fro, holding a piece of paper
against her chest, and when she was ready to begin again,
stopped, turned toward Fad, and cleared her throat.

"How are you, today, James?" she asked in a high, ar-
tificial voice.

Fad made a grunt.

"No," she said. "When a person asks 'How are you,' you must respond in kind. Do you know what 'in kind' means?"

"Mommy?" asked Fad.

"Yes?" she said encouragingly, bringing her big face down to his level and arranging her features in a mask of perfect attention. If there had been a way to somehow mechanically draw the words out of him, suck the vowels from sheer air, she would have done it.

"When Mr. Rudolph yelled at me four years ago, why did I feel my arms were ears?" he asked.

"Oh, honey," Harta said, frowning. "You really really *really* must concentrate. Now," she said, "let's try it again." She turned, paced, swiveled briskly. "I'm going to ask you a question, and I want you to give the kind of answer that is appropriate. Appropriate is a very very important word, because it is what the world is, outside our house."

Hunh, I thought.

"Okay?" she asked.

"I want everything to stay the same forever and ever. No movement!" he cried, placed his hand in his mouth and bit it passionately.

"Now," she went on, ignoring him, "how are you today, James?"

He looked up, saw me lounging in the doorway, and pointed a gnawed finger my way.

"Go way!" he shouted.

She turned and shook her head at me once, distinctly.

Leaving them with a tiny smile, I walked to my room, shouldered my way into the closet, brushed old camphorsmelling clothes out of the way, and applied my eye to a hole. Months before, I'd drilled through the wall of my closet as part of a larger project of sustained surveillance and, squinting now into the aperture, could make out a part of her arm, a swatch of his chest. There were bits of colors. Nonetheless, I could hear quite clearly.

"Okay," she was saying gaily, "let's try again. How are you?"

"Fine, but Mommy?"

"What."

"What's at where the train ends?"

"Oh, just concrete blocks and things. But we can talk more about that later. Okay!" She clapped her hands together. "Stand up."

He did.

"Let's say we're on the checkout line at the supermarket, and the girl says, 'Do you want green stamps?' What do you say?"

"The ones that I lick, Mommy?"

They had made a rainy-day sport of pasting yards of small stamps into special books that were grown thick, densely crusted with ladders of little S & H stamps. Value one mill. "Yes," said Harta, "those."

"I say sure!" cried Fad, "I say yes yes oh yes!"

"Quick now, you're at a restaurant, and the waitress comes over to you, and she says, 'What would you like today?' Okay?"

"Yeah!" Fad responded with huge enthusiasm.

"What do you say?" she asked.

"Pie and mints?"

"No, honey. You read the menu, and then you—oh, James, look, it's really quite simple. When people ask you questions, you have to respond to them in kind—to use that phrase again. You must say things that they themselves can respond to. It's like a dance, honey. You have to partner them."

Another silence, then, in which I saw her body crossing the room toward him.

"Partner them," she said faintly.

I saw her envelop him in some way, draw abnormally near. This was followed by a lengthy silence, during which I strained my ears to make out something. I thought—though I was equally certain it couldn't be true—that I heard the sound of Fad *drinking*. But that was impossible.

And yet after a further pause, there was the faintest noise of suction, as if breath was being laboriously drained into the air—or out of it.

"Mommy?" Fad whispered.

"What?" Her voice was tiny.

"Am I going away?"

Again a silence.

"If you work very very hard with me, now, you'll never have to leave this house. I promise you that James, my darling."

My knee began to hurt from crouching and I straightened up—at the very same moment hearing a sharp, stabbing intake of breath and Harta crying, "James, no!"

Then silence again. But it was a silence special somehow, fraught with buzzing details, pieces of exceedingly interesting possibility.

Creeping from the bedroom, I crossed two yards of cream deep-pile carpet like a pool of curdled milk, and stopped at the entrance to the room. Staring upon the scene, I could feel my throat contract.

Fad, cheeks puffed out, arms crooked, had stabbed his fingers deep into her hair and jerked it tight, drawing her entire scalp to a point and causing her herself, in some large horsey way, to stand nearly doubled over. On his face, small waves of happiness appeared to have risen, collided, and then frozen in place.

A tooth throbbed, it seemed right behind my eye. I put my hand to my mouth and stood in the doorway watching.

Fad cranked his arms inward toward his body and leaned back on his heels, causing Harta, obligingly, to tilt farther forward at the waist.

I was going to go forward, to interpose myself heroically between the two of them. But I thought I'd wait a second and let things ripen. In the meantime, I noticed her hair. It was spread out in a pretty peacock wedge display scattered through with lights, darks, and wonderful rich cinnamon accents.

"Stop it now," she whispered, though neither of them changed position or moved at all.

In my chest, a hot, sick signal began. I recognized its meaning: joy.

Fad cranked his arms harder, pulling them toward his chest and drawing Harta forward on her toes to expose the heart-shaped calf muscles in her legs that I loved, feet arched in dainty downward cramps, body tall as a tower.

From my illustrated book of tortures there came to mind the image of a man burned at the stake, watching the lower half of his body licked by dabbling twists of flame with an expression of divine mildness on his face. Such, I thought, is Fad.

"Gunnnh!" he gasped, unable to put his joy into words.

"Stop it *please*," said Harta.

"Honey?" called Max cheerily, from downstairs. "Did you get the mail?"

Her voice responded in absolute calm: "It's by the banister."

Fad, seeming not to like that, pulled harder still.

She took a large, shaky step forward.

She—let me make this clear—engulfed Fad, loomed over him, outweighed him by at least two to one. Easily, with no stretch at all, she could have reached out, opened her hands on his neck, chest, head, and squeezed the life out of him.

"Oh darling," she begged, helpless.

I took my hand out of my mouth just then, right around the moment she began to cry. Hitching my thumbs in my belt loops, I sauntered into the room with my chest puffed out.

Fad and Harta were by then too far gone to take notice of me. And so, unobserved, I reached out, teed off, and walloped Fad as hard as I could in the windpipe, having learned from Little League experience that this particular little zone was just perfect for disabling applications of force. Harta, released from his clutches, tumbled back toward the wall, while Fad, basically an enormous physical coward, started to cry—whooping, bowel-deep sounds like a police siren. At which point Harta, recovering her balance, came right back hard and fast—but not at Fad, no. At me! She cuffed me on the ear at the same moment as Max, alerted out of his benign, mail-reading haze by the sudden explosion of sounds, zoomed up the stairs, appeared at the doorway, surveyed the scene, and shook his head sorrowfully as he said, "I've told you a thousand times to leave your brother alone, but you just won't listen, will you? Well, you've really got it coming this time." There was the familiar long hiss of his belt being drawn from his trousers. Knowing better than to resist, I shut my eyes and faced the wall.

JULY

EIGHT

The rocket rose straight up as if thrilled. It lifted into the sky along a glowing stalk and then exploded in a puffball of fire that drooped hugely over everybody a moment before dwindling away into darkness. Another flew up and simply popped like a big flashbulb, which then rushed to touch your face a second later with the pressure-wave of its blast. And another sketched a series of lines in the air, like it was trying to connect the dots of outer space.

July Fourth had arrived. It was the time of year when we were supposed to be celebrating the fact that we'd beaten the English, and were trying to remember how great it was to be an American. We were supposed to know Revolutionary War dates and battles, but the main thing that stuck in my mind was that George Washington had wooden teeth, a girlish haircut, and surprised the drunken Hessian soldiers by crossing the Delaware River in a boat. Plus, he wore tights like a ballet dancer and never lied. Who cared? The main point was much simpler: Fireworks were simply one of the neatest, most amazing things in the entire world, and the real mystery was why they didn't have them every single night.

The sky flared and darkened above us, and between the

booms and blasts I took the time to make a quick private scan of our neighbors, who were assembled around me on picnic benches and folding chairs they had dragged into the middle of the street. I saw the Brillsteins, with Arnold, their bratty four-year-old, and, sitting next to them, the Cathcarts, who were as usual holding drinks in their hands. The Prines were on vacation, but I saw the Knoxes, Mr. and Mrs., both of whom were in their sixties and had perfect heads of white hair, like molded soap. Then, with an electric shock, I spotted Sabina Satiani, who I thought had been away and traveling with her family.

I was very excited to see her. Sabina Satiani lived directly around the corner from us and was the first completely perfect girl I'd ever known. Sabina was great. She was different. Harta called her "refined." Inexplicably arrived at our school from Italy the year before, she was politely poised and intricately perfumed. I knew, from having been in class with her, that her handwriting was composed of perfect little loops and the creases of her clothes were as sharp as blades.

Another thing about Sabina: When in her presence, the malice I felt toward everybody—and especially Fad—seemed to vanish on the spot. And I liked that.

I avoided her nervously for the rest of the evening, and scooted home as soon as possible. But the next morning, after thinking it over for hours, and trying out a hundred different tones and approaches in the air of the bathroom, I called her up, and simply said, "Hi." She greeted me with a noise of slowly shattering glass—"How are you" in her native language—and then after talking to me for a few minutes asked me to meet her for a picnic that afternoon at nearby Verona Lake. This had been beyond what I'd expected by about a hundred miles, and I hung up excitedly, washed my face, and set out.

The day was warm, but ever since the heat wave people seemed happy to be outdoors when the temperature was in the eighties, and the neighborhood was busy. We lived at the top of a long, steep hill, and walking down the hill was usually fun because every house you passed was set on its own little shelf, with its own little striped flower garden, black patch of driveway, and the pad of its front lawn, and as you went by you could pretend you were on an escalator gliding down past the floors of a giant department store. As I walked, sprinklers twirled their water-ropes on the grass. People in gloves and frightening clippers were at work boxing their hedges into funny angles, lawn mowers revolved around lawns, girls skipped rope. The air had a concentrated green smell of summer to it, and at a certain point, a plane from Teterboro Airport drifted by high above me, changing sound directly overhead as if falling asleep in the sky.

The day was sunny, but my mind was filled with endless dark thoughts. Take the smiling deliveryman who had recently arrived with a package for Harta—just why did he leave his truck, motor idling, in front of our stoop for a full five minutes? And the sewer repairman from the public works department with the big arms, to whom Harta slowly, incredibly slowly, gave a glass of apple juice beaded with coldness—he had winked at her in a certain way as he took the glass, did he think I didn't notice? A doctor had called the other day, and addressed her by her first name on the phone, and there had been a man at the gas station whose voice had turned thick like disgusting syrup as he took her money.

A pattern was developing, it seemed to me, and the pieces of that pattern pointed all in one direction.

Deep in the hot swirl of my thoughts, grinding my teeth, clenching my fists, I suddenly heard my name called by a familiar voice, and looked up, surprised, to see the oval of

Verona Lake glittering peacefully in front of me, and Sabina, on the grass, waving and smiling. I shook my head, and walked up casually and said hi. As soon as we were seated, I stared at her. Her eyes were bright green and almond-shaped. The dark bangs of her hair curled like twin commas around her pale face. Her mouth was moving. She was saying the word "Napoli." This was better than Harta, better than Fad, better by far than Max. As she talked, Sabina laid the lunch out on a tablecloth so that it looked like a miniature landscape: glittering sea of foil-wrapped potatoes, beach of roasted chicken, a forest of salted carrot sticks and celery. Then, suddenly, she stopped. Her face fell. She placed her hands in her lap.

"You look so sad," said Sabina.

"Me? Sad?"

"You look unhappy. You have the saddest look on your face."

She extended a long finger toward the carrot sticks.

"Don't you feel well? Eat a little bit, you'll feel better." Sabina spoke in the voice of a miniature lady, with an accent part British, part something else.

"I'm fine, Sabina. But things are weird back at, you know"—I jerked my head—"home."

"That's too bad," she said, reaching for the vegetables.

"Yeah, you know my brother?"

"Of course I know him, poor boy." Sabina opened her mouth, and with her little white teeth snipped the end off a carrot. "How is James?"

"Well, my mother's just started a new home training course with him, but that's not the real problem."

"No, what is?"

"I don't know, exactly. I just get this feeling like there's something else going on there."

"Where, Denny?"

"In the house, with my mom."

She sighed, and placed her hands together on her lap. Her brow furrowed. It seemed she was searching for the right thing to say. Sabina always said the exact right thing. "Did you know I have a cousin who is, retarded?" She smiled brilliantly. "His name is Luca and he has water on the brain or something. It's top secret, but they say his mother, my Aunt Isabella drinks too much."

"Really?" I cried, happy to have something in common with Sabina. "So does my dad! Is it gin or whiskey?"

But she only looked at me strangely a moment.

"Are you, uh," I said, "having a good summer?"

"So-so." She lowered her eyes from my face and poured lemonade into paper cups with a rattle. "We just got back from vacation on the island of Capri, which was beastly hot. Papa got cross and was a nasty man for two whole days. Later this summer we'll be going back to Italy to visit my older sister, Tatiana."

"Your sister? I didn't know you had a sister." I bit into the chicken—cool and thick.

"Yes, she's a very nice person and extremely beautiful. She is studying in Milan at the Politecnico."

"What's that?"

"Just a school."

"Where they invented polio?" I was trying hard to make her laugh, but instead, she studied me closely a second, and said, "Do you know, you are *sweating*."

"Am I?" I wiped my slick forehead with a napkin.

Sabina smiled. "Are you nervous or just hot?" she said.

"Well, it *is* hot today."

There was a pause of a few seconds, during which we both chewed our food. I tried to synchronize my jaw movements to hers, but she kept slowing down and speeding up.

Finally, concentrating hard, I got it exactly right, and our mouths moved in the very same small kneading motions for about five seconds. It was like kissing her without her knowing it, I thought. It was like making out through sheer air. It was like—but then she stopped chewing. Her mouth opened.

"Would you like to know about my boyfriends in Italy?" she asked.

"Well—"

"I had many," she said. "Some were very rich, and some were very cute. But I wasn't serious about them. Can I tell you why?"

"Yes," I said.

"Because I spent most of my time in the Sacred Heart School, with the nuns. I read the Bible lots. It's a very serious and beautiful book that was dictated directly from the mouth of God. Do you know what the word *undefiled* means?"

"No."

"It means pure, pure enough to enter Heaven. I'm thinking of going to a convent school in Berne, which is in Switzerland, where you wear flannel robes and pray six times a day. I've been assured it's a super-lative experience."

"A what?" I asked, dropping my eyes to the ground where I saw a bug, antennae buzzing, attempting to scale a nearby grass blade.

"It means a good thing to do," said Sabina. She cleared her throat. "The nuns say that religion makes us ask the important questions."

The bug made it to the top of a grass blade and looked around.

"Questions?" I said. "Like, what questions?"

"Listen," she said, with a show of patience, "you know where you live, right?"

"Sure, Forty-four Drainer Drive."

"Okay, but do you know *why* you live there? Can you tell me why, in the deepest sense, you were chosen to live in that particular place?"

I thought a second.

"West Caldwell," I said, groping, "was too expensive?"

Sabina frowned. "You're quite missing the point," she said. "There are no accidents in life, Denny. Someone's always watching over your shoulder, even when you're sneezing or snorkeling or riding on a plane. At the top of the sky is a room, and in that room are a billion souls floating around and looking back down at the earth and at everything you do. A soul is like a balloon with a candle in it. The priests explained it all to me this summer." We sat and looked at the pond a while in silence. It was green and had the authority of something at least a million years old. Suddenly I heard myself saying, "You're great."

"What?"

"No, I mean you're so smart and beautiful that I have to tell you, you're just a great person."

She laughed a tittering soft laugh, like a handful of sand tossed at a cymbal. "Sometimes I wish you could tell my mother that. I'm not sure she'd agree."

I laughed, heard myself laughing (a gobbling, hungry sound), and stopped. I stared at her hand a second, and then, suddenly inspired, said, "Can I ask you something?"

"Yes, Denny?"

"Your skin. Does it ever gross you out you can see the veins?"

NINE

Did Harta know I was drawing near her secret life? Suddenly she began coming to my room at night, arriving always at that moment when I lay balancing on the sheer edge of sleep. Clad only in a nightgown, with her hair pinned in an soft auburn crown on her head, she glided to the side of my bed, sat down beside me, and rubbed her hands along the wings of my back. Her breath, a flower of milk in the air, enveloped my face. In a low murmuring voice she began talking compulsively, lavishly, recounting fantastic stories of men carried away by high winds, drowned at sea, eaten by wild animals; of the old country across the sea, where pious people lived in villages the color of mud. The other thing she did was talk incessantly about Max. I thirsted for the information.

"Did you know a millionaire proposed to me once?" she asked, fingering my curls.

"Oh, yeah?" I liked the sound of the word *millionaire*.

"He was an older man, but if I'd've married him I would have had the world at my feet."

"What does that mean, the world at your feet?"

"Do anything you want, have anything you want. Honey, you know what it means?"

"What?" Listlessly, I toyed with my pillow.

"It means happiness, baby. It means money money money!"

"Oh, that's nice. But Mommy?"

"Yes?"

"How did you meet Dad?"

"How did I meet your father?" There was a cooling, a literal cooling of her voice.

"We met at a beach club—like the kind of place we're going to next weekend."

"Did you like him?"

"What a silly question—of course I liked him. He was so . . . so handsome, with his cleft chin and his dark eyes and gentle way of talking. All the girls were wild over him."

"And then what?"

"Aren't we curious. 'Then what?' What do you think, you nosy thing? Then we got married, of course!"

"And what about your other boyfriends?"

"My what?" I felt, rather than saw, her rear back in the dark.

"Your other boyfriends, like Salvatore Tinello and Eugene Feigen and Jeffrey Gleiner," I said calmly, referring to the men with whom I had seen Harta linked arm-in-arm in photographs I'd retrieved from a box on the top shelf of her closet—dark, beefy men in bathing suits who smiled at the camera with revolting candor while touching Harta with their fingers at the elbow and waist. She had written their names on the backs of the photos.

"I'll—how did you?" She laughed nervously. "When did . . ." There was a pause. Harta's hands were suddenly on the nape of my neck, where she began to caress me carefully, deliberately. The sensation was immediately hypnotic. I wanted suddenly to roar like a tiger, because it was then, on the jumbled edge of sleep, that I understood at last: It was not those men, it was me! Me who would live with Harta forever and ever! Me who would be her hero and do heroic, important things for her, like falling out of planes and being captured by the enemy! Passionately she would feed me tuna fish sandwiches with those sour little droppings called capers in them. And just as passionately an understanding would arise between us, an understanding at whose very center something striking and unthinkable would begin to happen. I looked forward to it all keenly, especially the unthinkable part.

But now Harta was saying, "Ah, Denny, it's hard to explain the way things go between men and women . . . but people have to make adjustments. That is, that when a man loves a woman and a woman a man, when people who are close . . . oh, I'm not clear."

"Isn't marriage forever until you die?"

"Yes, it is." Her hands, abandoning all pretense, were now working hard on the sleep-nodes of my neck. I struggled to stay awake. "It is, but not always. Everybody wants to stay together, you see. But sometimes things happen. . . ."

"Like what?"

"Well, people fall in and out of love, people die, people move on. Imagine being in the same homeroom class for your entire life."

"Yuccch!"

"Even if you loved Mrs. McGlade very much, you'd still want to move on when it came time to change grades."

"Mrs. Mazzelli!" I cried, thinking of the buxom teacher with whom I had once inadvertently collided while waiting on line for an assembly. Her body billowed around me, causing a strangely pleasant sensation I couldn't put my finger on.

"Exactly. So that most times, though people stay married forever and ever, there are times"—it seemed to me her voice grew slightly huskier—"when people have to do things to save their own lives."

"Do you love Daddy now?"

The hands on my neck stopped. After a moment, they started again.

"Sweetie, of course I do." The hands were now digging deep into the rocky rim of my skull where it met the neck. I felt sleep as a kind of gas, a black gas filling my head. Harta knew exactly what she was doing.

"And you wouldn't have a boyfriend when you have a husband like Daddy, right?"

"Of course not, what a silly thought. Sometimes, Denny, you say the strangest things. Do you have a confession you want to make?" she asked. "Is there something you want to tell me?"

Sleep, in heavy waves dispatched from a dark sea, began rolling into my head. With difficulty I kept breathing, fought to keep my nostrils over the warm, smothering seawater. To my amazement, I could breathe even once my mind slipped below the surface. It was calm and peaceful there, as I imagined it was inside Harta's body. A steep wave lifted me up into the air. I heard her say, "Confess all, you little Romeo. You're in love with Sabina," and then I plunged deep into the water, out of sight and sound. With an enormous heave, I surfaced one last time, and from my momentary height I thought I saw her crouching at the door, saying in a rapid whisper, "Remember this, darling. Your father is a cad. He takes from my most vulnerable places, and gives nothing back." Then a wave fell on me and rushed away with the rest of my mind.

TEN

I n my daily log, I noted:

> *Subject A is exhibiting a huge increase in strange behavior. She's wearing lots of makeup, changing her hairstyle every week, and her voice when we eat at the table is loud all the time now, like she's shouting, pretending she is happy which she probably is not.*
>
> *Subject B is looking sleepy these days. I clocked him returning to the house from his car in the driveway, and he took six more steps than usual and was almost one and a half times as slow as the week before. In technical terms, this is called "a loss of efficiency." Also, he almost fell over in the vicinity of the laundry room last week, but he caught himself at the last minute. Liquor was smelled on his breath for 164 days in a row, so far. I know what it smells like because I'm trained.*

On July 12, at 8:15 A.M., in the midst of a sunny morning, Max
and Harta officially stopped kissing each other good-bye. I noticed immediately, because no matter how tense things had
been in the house, they had always gone through the act of tilting their heads toward one another and making sounds. But
suddenly that morning there were no nuzzles, smacking gob-
bles, nor even the dry pecks with which they sometimes used
to bracket the beginning and end of certain days. Their hands,
which had occasionally finished gestures in each other's hair,
remained stiffly at their sides. They said good-bye using the
formal series of bows and flourishes with which once, on edu-
cational TV, I had watched a bullfighter salute the crowd.

And then he got impaled.

I stood by as they turned coldly away from each other,
and walked in opposite directions, Harta going upstairs, Max
moving quietly down the hall and closing the door behind him
with a strange gentleness. When he was gone, I sat a moment
in the kitchen and came to a momentous decision: I would
open up a new notebook dedicated entirely to my father.

I already knew some things about Max. I knew that he
had $2,900 in his savings account, and that if he and Harta
"predeceased" me, a man named Randolph Chapman would
be my guardian. I knew that Max drove 6.4 miles to work at
his office, where he sat behind the glass-topped acreage of his
desk or walked up and down aisles of piled machinery, bark-
ing orders, waving a cigar. I knew that he spent his time at
home either sitting in his study or crouched in the basement
in front of his workbench, holding small silver tools in his
hands, tightening screws, placing jointed angles together
along straight edges. At such moments, wearing a leather
apron, he searched the winding roads of wires to their sources,
brought the hot, healing tip of his soldering iron down. A drift

of smoke uncurled upward in the air. The connection was made. The radio played "The Hit Parade" again; the bicycle wheel spun; the refrigerator, with a thump, lurched back to life.

Max, smiling. spread his arms wide, letting his rage drop away. It was like the sun breaking through a weeklong lid of clouds. Max was always angry. Rust, racism, late bills, rain in the sky—these things seemed to have leaked out of the world and settled in his face, in its harshness, its strange darkness, and the fact that, when seen in profile, it was notched like a key.

Another thing I knew was that Max was so angry all the time in part because he was something called a Marxist. This meant that he suffered more than other people, because he believed in beautiful words like *justice* and *education*, and understood that the Vietnam War, as he said at dinner, was "one of the most barbaric in the history of American colonialist expansion." It meant that whenever he was in the mood, Max might be counted on to unravel even the most apparently happy headline back to some hard, cruel fact of nastiness. A series of old German books high on his shelf was the key. It was because of them that he could rant to guests about the lies of Lyndon Johnson, or rail at me against "those fools in Washington, dupes of big business, you understand?"

Marxism, it quickly became clear to me, was a philosophy that allowed you to be thoughtful and furious all day long.

I stood in the kitchen, drummed my fingers on a nearby shelf, and wondered if maybe, just possibly, another of the reasons for my father's steady, burning, murderous rage might lie within a small footlocker in a storage shed behind the house. The footlocker, Harta had once told me, was full of papers about Max's experience in "the war."

The war.

It had been explained to us in school as something started by the Japanese, pursued by the Germans, and ending when America dropped the fizzing white exclamation point of an atom bomb on Hiroshima. Max had told me that the Second World War had "remade the world." He said that it had been the "last good war," and that he had enlisted over the objections of his entire family. His face, however, grew pinched, tense, fierce with a strain of nerves when I pressed him for details of his role in the fighting. If I pressed further, he stood up, yelled angry words at me, and stalked off in a fury.

It was time to find out a little bit more about this war.

Climbing to the top of the stairs, I took a quick reading on the house: father long gone to work; mother and brother in brother's bedroom, singing "Edelweiss" together, their voices climbing tiredly up the chorus of the song. When they hit the high note, I rushed back down the stairs. My destination was the booming old grandfather clock, which contained a special shelf within it where Max kept his ring of "secret keys"—to spring the locks of his study, his car, and, I suspected, his footlocker. Standing on a kitchen chair, I retrieved the keys, and after assuring myself that the voices upstairs were still grinding along in their song, I stole out to the backyard shed where the footlocker was kept. The door of the shed opened silently, giving up a blast of warm, kept air and revealing boxes of old tools sitting in ragged rows: big black pipes that looked like they'd belonged to a steamship, a brass clock, a large compass with a cracked glass and all its inner-eye liquid drained out, and, in the far corner, the trunk. Three keys in a row went into the big padlock before the fourth one worked, the metal sprang open with a squeak, and I lifted the heavy wooden lid of the trunk to stare amazed at a wealth of browning photographs, rubber-banded stacks of letters, clippings from newspapers, tiny medals in grooved velvet boxes, and a series of spiral notebooks with the words *Journal* printed on their covers in soft faded pencil. It was clear that this entire small city of details, times, and places added up, collectively, to something like the truth. I opened up the journals, began to read. Leafing slowly through the books, devouring Max's detailed accounting, I released tiny puffs of mildewed dust as I went. I was eager to watch it happening, unable to believe that all these ancient facts, salted randomly over the hundreds of pages, could fuse into a single, unforgettable image of Max himself, younger, leaner, a navigator in a gray uniform, sitting inside a B-24 "Liberator" bomber, and looking up wide-eyed as the attack began.

The German fighters flung sunlight from their wings, came in fast and hard from above and shook his plane with stupendous concussions. Sirens, deep-throated, screamed. Immediately two of the four engines stopped. Max glanced out the smeary plastic window of his nacelle—not frightened so much as he was stunned by the sight of a delicate propeller stilled, motionless in midair. A sudden roil of black smoke belched from the wall, accompanied by a hiss and the sight of a sheaf of pencils sliding slowly off the table and drumming with tiny clinks on the riveted metal floor.

The plane plunged steeply downward. Max levered himself effortfully onto his feet, and looked again out the window. I looked too. The Messerschmitts were spread out below us in perfect formation like a smattering of little cusped leaves floating in the blue water of sky, wheeling. Occasionally tiny

*sputtering flashes were visible hatching from be-
neath their wings.*

*A boll of smoke uncurled upward, dense and
acrid. Max coughed as I grabbed him by the shoulders of his flight suit and drew him forward and
into the main cabin.*

*There the air was clear. We had the sense of
changing atmospheres. And with it the feeling that
perhaps it had all been a dream. Everything was
still utterly calm here. Along the curved dashboard
the needles of gauges floated stably against their
sweeps of numbers. The warping sound of the engines rose steadily up through the bones of our legs.
The sky was blue. The neat, calm arrangements of
papers and machinery seemed to assert that everything was fine, that perhaps we had simply unnec-
essarily panicked.*

*The pilot's head was exploded. Against one
wall of the cabin brain matter had been flung as if
from a rinse cycle. Gouts of blood were still running
down a side window. Max and I bent closer, willing
our eyes to focus. The pilot's flying suit, strapped
to its seat, was left untouched and mounted neatly
to the gaping stalk of bone where his head had
been.*

*The copilot whistled. I turned. The copilot,
a man our own age, sat staring straight ahead with
eyes shut, whistling cheerfully. When Max touched
him on the shoulder he screamed "NO!" once, gigantically, and then shut his eyes again and resumed his whistling. It was Old MacDonald Had
a Farm, the first verse repeated again and again
and again. Leaning forward in the plunging,*

*smoking plane, Max fumbled with the clasps and
detached the man from his seat belt. The copilot
had stopped on a single high, violently blown note
and begun crying, eyes jammed shut. Gently, in the
ever more steeply downtilting fuselage, we lifted
the man from his seat, and pulled him toward the
door.*

*Max opened the emergency exit, jerking the
huge handle to. The noise of war rode into the plane,
along with a wind that took our breath away.*

*C'mon, Max shouted, away we go! Jack, he
said, please you must! A sharp odor filled the com-
partment. The man had soiled himself. Okay, he
said, and dragged the man across the metal floor
and got him to the edge of the door, where the man
came suddenly and spectacularly alive.*

*I can't! he screamed, flailing his arms and
shrinking back against my father.*

No, Max said, regretfully, the fact is you can.

*Max pushed him once, hard, in the center of
the back and the copilot tilted into the onrushing
air and was snapped away into the vault of space.
Falling away into smallness, he spread his arms
and legs outward and then held them there, as if
to brace himself against the idea of endless atmosphere.*

*Pull the cord, Max muttered to himself,
standing still in the plane and adjusting his own
parachute. I followed his lead. All around us we
saw drifting long-waisted blooms of flak. Below,
the ground was rapidly becoming detailed. Trees,
the lingual stripe of a road, a park. Wafer-thin
people promenading.*

Grab the cord and pull it, schmuck, Max muttered to himself, positioning his toes on the edge of the door, for a moment resisting the terrible suck of the wind. The parachute below us opened with its miraculous perfect tented silk apparition and, reassured, he jumped.

If you, the flight instructor had said, *have the presence of mind to retain your rip cord handle during a real jump in combat, send it to me after the war and I'll send you back fifty dollars.*

A terrific jerk snapped white through the bones of his body, drew the sight from his eyes and jammed his ears. He announced he was going to faint, and began to say so to the deepening darkness when suddenly, miraculously, a tree of energy rose up through his nerves and he was alert again, in midair, he was walking gigantically down the sky again, calmly, he was a man beneath a white sail, a billowing canopy, with the sunshine out, the taste of sweet oxygen in his mouth, and his hair, it seemed to him, literally hissing on his head.

The same thing happened to me.

We stowed our handles. The high altitude sun felt strong. The air was blue and the horizon curved away, with little bumps and inlets for cities. Slightly off to one side, rushing amidst foothills, a river glinted like the edge of a coin.

I had always wanted to be with Max like this, simple, easy, man to man. I was so glad it was happening at last. Drifting, we felt the heat of the sun on our faces. The chutes tugged heavily around our chests and under our arms. We pulled a cord *to attempt to turn, desiring to make for a large clearing on the far side of a river, but we were unable to affect the progress of our fall.*

Max noticed he was bleeding. His hand, wiping his face, came away stained bright red. I bent closer to look. It was okay, nothing serious. The ground, meanwhile, proceeded upward at speed, specifics looming of texture and detail, the herringbone of ditches and orchards. As we arrived at treeline the earth widened toward its horizons like a carpet unrolling at impossibly high speed. We hit the ground hard, crumpled as taught in an end over end roll, and then with the taste of grass in our face and our ankles throbbing, stood, stowed our blowing chutes, and looked around.

We had landed in a park. We had somehow, incredibly, touched down in the center of a local greensward. Elderly persons stood frozen in midgape. Children, appalled, sobbed out loud. Summoning our presence of mind, we buried our dog tags, stood up. We had fallen like a twin-headed god from the sky, and perhaps we could turn this imperial moment to our own benefit somehow. We spread our arms and smiled.

Nazis, firing over our heads, burst from the woods.

I lurched forward from my stool and fell onto the floor with a musical crash of memorabilia. I was dizzy, light-headed, maybe just a little sick. The journal ended there, and I had been drawn so deeply into the detail of Max's words and descriptions that I'd forgotten where or who I was. What had the

Nazis done to him? Why had Max never told me about any of this? Why had I only been told he'd "served in the war" and been kept in the dark about something this major and great?

I sat waiting for him all afternoon with a hot feeling in my heart. A war hero for a father! I wanted to rush to him and hug him hard. I wanted to whisper into his ear the precious secret that would protect him from his wife. I wanted to be his son forever and ever. No wonder he was so moody, so silent! The door swept open at exactly 5:15, and Max entered the living room, winking at me from above the boxy blue suit he wore, that crackled, in winter, with a tiny violence when he moved. This was called static electricity—bizarre. He rolled his bloodshot eyes in an alert circuit around the house, checking for Harta, and then from within his blazer withdrew a beautiful silver pocket flask, which rose slowly in the air, redoubling the light from the starburst fixture overhead. The cords in his throat stood out a moment, his Adam's apple jogging.

"That's better," he said with a sigh, wiping his mouth with the back of his hand. "How's everything, Columbus? Where's your mother?"

"Daddy," I said, feeling my lower lip trembling, "I have something I want to say to you."

"Right," said Max, ignoring me and going to look out the window at the backyard. He put his hands on his hips. "Gosh," he muttered, "look at that zoysia grass grow."

Zoysia grass was a special superresistant strain of lawn that had been made by scientists in the cool white light of their laboratories, dribbling liquids into glassware. It arrived in a special package, with a special shovel, and you punched plugs of it into the lawn. The plugs were then to grow up and merge by expanding radially outward in every direction—a special process. But the merge had never taken place and the lawn was now starred with patches of luxuriant thriving zoysia grass, dark emerald against the dimmer shade of green.

"Daddy, I read a thing about the war that—"

"Want to play catch?" Max interrupted me, knocking back the flask again and taking a big gulp. Catch was a rare offer, a very rare offer, but before I could decide, there was a disturbance on the stairs. Fad walked into the very center of the room and stood there in his accustomed posture. His shoulders were narrow and his hair leaped evenly away from his skull in every direction, and with great and impressive slowness, an eye turned off-center in his head.

"What's that, Daddy?" he asked.

"It's called a pocket flask," said Max, "and it's man's best friend."

Fad smiled—though only momentarily. His mouth closed down and he made a thoughtful sound, puffing air through the loop of a vowel. I'd long ago given up wanting to comment on this, to attract attention to it, to point it out to myself as an oddity. Fish with barred lightnings on their sides breathing inexplicably in water—now *that* was amazing.

"Catch now," said Max, "or forever hold your mitt."

I suddenly felt tired, enormously tired. The drama of the war discoveries had inflated me with love for Max. But his drunken refusal to allow me to present my feelings left me frazzled and small. Excluded. A familiar sensation.

"Nah," I said, "I've got work to do."

"Work?"

"Yeah, filing and things."

"Filing, at your age?" He looked me in the eye for the first time that evening. "What, like your nails?" I walked away with loud, hooting waves of his laughter breaking against my back as I climbed the stairs and went to my room to lie down.

ELEVEN

Perhaps, I asked myself when I was feeling calmer, the problem was not people, but words. Words like *war* and *peace*, *marriage* and *divorce*; words that as you shot them out of the gun of your mind turned into the letters b-u-l-l-e-t and made you bleed. In a book like Max's journal, even the parts of speech were dangerously alive. Grabby purchase of nouns and verbs, pins-and-needles spice of punctuation, the neon heat of the adjective—I was amazed at the ease with which adults flung the coiling ropes of phrases from their mouths, with no thought of what might happen as a result. To me, peril waited in the very next utterance. In the word that might drop clear off the edge of the earth. In the searched-for thought that could escape from the tip of your tongue, drift into the sun, and blind you for life.

Derwent, I knew, was master of a parallel system—organic chemistry, that universe of endless chain-link diagrams. But words were odder, sloppier, more powerful by far. You could write the word *die* in an empty room and cause a person in a story a year later to pitch forward, lifeless, into his pea soup. You could write *fly* and a billion geese would obediently lift from the ground, with honks and the roar of a great wind rising. When scientists dove to the molten middle of the earth, or flew to the remote sphere of the moon, or broke the racing electron to bits, I was certain that what they would find was not minerals, or matter, or atoms, but words.

Formed in the voice of Harta.

"So, sonny boy, are you happy to be going to the beach for the week?" She had turned from the front seat of the car and was addressing me.

"No." I looked away from her and at the familiar houses of our neighborhood, wedge-shaped, crayon-colored, slipping by in reverse as we drifted down the hill,

"What a sourpuss you're turning into, Mr. Secret Agent," Harta said, turning forward, as if in reproach. After a moment, she turned back. "How can you not like a week at the beach, Denny? The sea, the sand, the sunshine. The clouds make these special patterns over the ocean, like nowhere else. And wait until you see the beautiful hotel your father reserved for us. Your pappy's in a spare-no-expense state of mind! Sometimes I wonder what's gotten into the man." She turned to him. "Tell us, did you win the lottery, honey? Did you break the bank at Monte Carlo?"

Max said nothing at all. Harta turned back to me, and put her hands on either side of her mouth.

"Don't mind him, he's counting his money," she whispered, and then burst into giggles.

I forced a tiny smile to make her happy. I didn't want to go the beach. I didn't want to go anywhere at all. I resented even leaving the house, if Fad was in tow, and for good reason. Invariably, he did something spectacular, embarrassing, humiliating to my sense of the occasion. Just as invariably this provoked what I had secretly come to call That Way—a certain mix of sympathy and secret amusement on the part of onlookers that made me crazy. I had grown used to the nudges, the pointed fingers, the jerks of the head and widening eyes of people around us, but for the life of me I couldn't stifle the anger that accompanied them. Harta and Max didn't seem to notice, or at least pretended not to. And so it was left to me, traveling as if in another, dirtier little room a foot away from my parents, to gather the scorn and humiliation and store it away. I dreamed often of carrying a handheld sign, to be used wherever I happened to be loitering in public with my family, and bearing the following message:

THIS BOY IS ONLY INCIDENTALLY RELATED TO THE
FUNNY-LOOKING PEOPLE SITTING OR STANDING NEXT
TO HIM, AND IN PARTICULAR TO THE TALL GAWKY ONE
WHO IS JUMPING UP AND DOWN, SHOUTING, FARTING,
BURPING, OR BITING HIS HAND. HE HAS A GOOD SIDE-
ARM CURVEBALL AND CORRESPONDS WITH AT LEAST
TWO LEARNED SOCIETIES. TALK TO HIM, GET TO KNOW
HIM, ENJOY THE SURPRISING PLEASURE OF HIS COM-
PANY.

Two hours after our departure from the house, we arrived at Sandy Hook. The cars were backed up nearly to the turnpike, a shimmering chrome river of Cadillac Eldorados and Chevrolet Biscaynes. We bumped our way slowly to the hotel and checked into our room, and finally, by noon, we were on the beach, watching the ripples slither up the sand. Fad and I sat at the water's edge, while Max, up the beach, smoked a Cuesta-Rey cigar and read the paper with an expression of deep indigestion. Harta, as far as I could tell, was fast asleep under an umbrella. I took a moment out to stare at the ridged endless water. Waves were arriving from around the world and falling at my feet, long-backed curl after curl, ledge after toppling ledge. I dabbled my toes in the chilly foam and, lifting my eyes, realized with a start that the sky was just a reversed model of the ocean, and where there were birds above, drifting in air, below us there were fish with lidless eyes, hung like fruit in Jell-O.

When the sun went down, we returned to our beachfront rooms, showered off, and then drove to what Harta called a "luxe" restaurant. This was a big, airy space crowded with potted plants, driftwood logs, and giant sticks of bronze and glass that hung like smashed stars from the ceiling and sprinkled the tablecloths and floor with drops of light. The point of the decoration seemed to be that something precious might fall on you. If I let my eyes droop a little and looked through my lashes it was all flame-colored, silky, faintly dangerous.

I opened my eyes wide. Tall, pretty people were prettily spooning in their food, wittily going about having lives. Smoke drifted from their mouths in sideways clouds and I was in love with this shining vision of elegance.

The waitress came to our table and took our order as if it were the very thing that would most make her happy in life. Her plastic name tag read LURLEEN, and her hair was molded in the exact shape of the Liberty Bell. I was in love with Lurleen, too, and smiled at her in a way meant to indicate our togetherness in this perfect moment.

In a rare moment of public pleasure, Harta and Max sighed happily and raised their drinks as the tomato soup arrived. Max seemed suddenly to glow with satisfaction. He looked at me from across the table, and gave me a friendly nod. Harta, patting her hair for a moment, gradually let herself be drawn into a girlish smile. I felt the noise die down around us in the restaurant, as if the flame of the family, beginning to burn, had drawn a silent shawl of happiness around us. I scanned the area. No one was looking. Max told a dirty joke about gorillas and Frenchmen, which I didn't understand. Harta laughed—I mean, she really laughed. Fad, with his fake dead smile on his face, sat rocking to and fro, mildly distracted.

For a moment, stunned, I was given a look into what things must have been like when Max first met Harta and the simple, pretty thing in the air between them began to flower. Max, when he wanted to, could make a ray come out of his face that was as irresistible as music. I had watched him hold a roomful of people in the palm of his hand while telling a story. I had seen how he used to make Harta scream with laughter like blowing bubbles, chains of linked happy laughs floating up into the summer sky. I remembered those times. I loved Max. I loved Harta.

I climbed from my happy dream back down into my body and looked out at my brother sitting across from me, waving a half-eaten hand in front of his mouth and getting ready to speak. Did I love Fad? There was whitish junk gathered in the corners of his mouth. Some of this was crusted also in his nose.

"I think," he said, "I'd like to be an ant."

"Would you?" said Max cheerily. "Well, in the meantime, please pass the bread. Doesn't this soup smell great, honey?"

Harta nodded, smiling, and raised her spoon.

"Ants always know just what to do," Fad continued in a rising voice, "and they have a very good time, especially when no one sees them. At night they sleep without moving. Is that a thing to know? Dad?"

"What?"

"What would you do if you had an ant in your head?"

Max turned to look at him. His face had a pair of low-slung bags beneath the eyes.

"Just steady down now, dear," he said.

"But what would you do? Daddy you can't sit eating your soup with an ant crawling around in your head!"

"Can't we just enjoy our food without worrying about the ants," said Harta mildly.

"Or if it was in my ear?" he cried. "Then what?"

"You're retarded," I whispered out the side of my mouth, staring at a far corner of the room.

"Mommy!" exploded Fad. "He said I was retarded!"

He flung his spoon down into the bowl of soup in a way that made the contents stand up a moment in large red arrows before falling down all over the tablecloth.

Max sprang to his feet, and stabbed his forefinger in the air. "Denny to the car and now!" he shouted into the suddenly still air of the dining room.

In the remaining days at the beach, Fad, under my subtle coaching, repeatedly "acted out," as I heard Harta call it— throwing things, shouting things, and causing repeated applications of That Way from fellow diners, beach walkers, and confused lifeguards. It troubled me, but I had decided to override my public embarrassment for the sake of getting Fad into a hole too deep for him ever to climb out of.

To do that I had to use words again. Nasty, pelletlike words that when I spoke them left the taste in my mouth of old pennies. And yet—a small confession—I liked it. I enjoyed the flavor of being mean. It seemed to me a daring, refined thing that was something else besides: a force for truth. The naked hatred I sent out from beneath my grin was actually a desire that the world as I knew it might change, under the pressure of my nastiness, and in so doing drop a significant portion of its civilized façade and expose its big, dirty ass.

After six days, the prompting of several delicious ex-

plosions on Fad's part, and the return of loaded tension between Max and Harta, we left, vacation over, and arrived home
to a crashing surf of words: flyers advertising Electric Field
Therapy and Tibetan Mental Secrets and Placental Injections,
and a series of pamphlets about "therapeutic communities"—
Harta's last, best hope for Fad if he had to leave home after
all. The therapeutic communities often had creepy names—
Crestmere, Wryneck Heights, Ramphill Village—and their
brochures, to me, seemed bent on masking an essential secret.
Rivers of bright, sparkling words flowed across the pages,
forming tributaries that discussed tennis courts and horses,
greenhouses, orchards, and cows, in such happy language that
if you blinked, even once, you'd forget the main fact: that the
place was full of people with funny faces, many of whom could
barely eat their food, remember what day it was, or the name
of planet Earth.

Along with these brochures there was a single crisp,
precisely addressed envelope from the state. I plucked it from
Harta's bedside drawer and found out that a new commissioner of mental health by the name of Kroll had decided to
"tighten the definitional categories of all those children falling
under Phase Six domestic subsidies." In addition, he informed
her, there was something called the Comprehensive Exam—
a day-long session of interviews and tests for the entire family,
which would be administered a few weeks away on September
10, and that had as its goal a "conclusive determinant index
rating of the patient's ability to function effectively within the
family constellation." There were thick, throbbing, dangerous
words, which ran together, one after the other, like the string-
course of bricks around a building, and threatened somehow,
even sitting in quiet rows on the page.

TWELVE

I began listening in with even greater attention to Harta's phone calls with doctors—calls that increasingly ended with abrupt hang-ups on Harta's part that exploded in my ear like bombs. I watched her blue book fill with a rush of new notations on Fad's behavior, bits of encouragement to herself (*Concentrate!* was a recurrent favorite) and—a recent twist—pieces of relevant magazine articles torn out and glued into place. One page was devoted entirely to the following bit of print ripped from *Psychology Today*: "Mental health specialists have been all too quick to embrace the dogma that a child's emotional withdrawal and ego disorganization can be traced to parental behavior." This was customized by Harta with an exclamation point the size of a club.

On the next page was an entire paragraph torn from what seemed to be *Life* magazine, and enclosed in a cage of blue Magic Marker:

> During Biblical times, such children were often taken to healers who attempted to "cast out evil spirits," or "cleanse them." During Greek and Roman times, such children were occasionally sewed

into the wet skin of a goat, in an attempt to calm their strange behavior. The goat skin, as it dried and shrank, served as a forerunner of the strait-jacket. <u>During the entire pre-Christian era, when the healers failed, and when fear, force, and inflicted pain failed, abandonment became the final treatment method.</u>

Harta had underlined the last sentence so hard the pen had broken through the paper.

And then there were the home lessons. In the days after our return from the beach, they doubled, then tripled, in frequency. I heard their voices regularly from my closet—a soft, tranced, sealike murmuring, as if a giant cowrie shell had been dropped in there among my corduroys and cleated baseball shoes, importing the sound of the Asbury Park surf. To keep up with my increased surveillance responsibilities, I dragged a blanket and pillow into the closet and arranged them as a bed so that I could sleep there if necessary. This bed was soon surrounded with a sea of orange peels, erasers, notebooks, and pencils. I liked being in this closet better than I did in the world, where anything could happen at any given moment. In the warm dark of the closet, after all, only one thing could happen, and it happened over and over and over again.

"It's called a part," she said softly, holding a comb over Fad's unruly mop of hair and drawing a thin line down the center. With the edge of one hand, she ironed the heavy, lustrous fall of his curls one way, and then the other. He now had a center part through his hair, a style that gave him the faintly comic look of a singer in a barbershop quartet. Indifferent to this grooming, he sat biting his lips quietly, and occasionally flaring his nostrils.

"Every morning, like just about every other boy on the planet, you have to go into the bathroom, put a little water on your hair, and draw the comb through it to make this part, okay?" said Harta. Smiling, she dipped water from a green ceramic bowl and sprinkled drops of it on his head, massaging the roots of his hair as she went along. He groaned softly, and then, his breath catching on a sharp intake, said, "But what about the planes?"

"What planes are those, darling?" She was now smoothing the curls behind his ears, and then, crouching in front of him and holding him by the chin, surveying the results of her work.

"You know, you might look a bit better parted on the side. Do you like the thought of that, you little rake?"

Fad perked up at this.

"Am I a rake? Is that a good thing to be?"

"It just means a fancy man, honey. Do you feel like a fancy man?"

"Mommy I want to go on the planes. They go up and up and up. Do they ever just go away?"

She took out an atomizer and began soaking the front of his head with little puffs of mist. Drawing the comb through the wet hair, she smoothed the unruly licks and knobs with small pushes of her fingers, and then, with a deft slicing motion, divided his hair on one side. "Here," said Harta, pursing her lips as she molded his hair. "You now look like a perfectly distinguished young gentleman."

Sighing, she squatted down to his level. I watched through the hole in my closet as she smoothly lowered herself to the ground, her enormous legs drawing up on either side in the manner of a kangaroo, splaying open her woman's organ, if Derwent was correct, like the oval rubber change purse in which she kept nickels and dimes.

I felt the muscles of my jaw slacken. She was doing something to Fad's face but her body blocked my view. I thought I saw her moisten her finger and then apply it to him. "Now," she said, "after you have made a—what it is called?"

"Party."

"No, James, a part. After you have made a part, you have to brush your teeth, every morning. You have beautiful clean white teeth, and you probably don't realize how lucky you are to not have braces, either."

"Daddy was in a plane once, he said so, and then the plane went down. Mommy stop!"

"No," she said, determined, "this is important. Your teeth must be brushed every morning."

"Gobby, bob id!"

"I won't stop it till we've cleaned out all the disgusting cake and junk you have stored in here. My God, I think I see M and M's, and there's a Hershey bar. Here's a . . . yuccch! What is this?"

She reared back, allowing me to see that she was actually brushing his teeth with her index finger, cranking it in small circles around the inside of his mouth. The same bowl from which she drew the water for his hair she now swished the finger in. Swishing it and then applying toothpaste, she said,

"You know, I have a mind to give that Dr. Yampolsky a chewing out. He's left all kinds of stuff in your mouth. I see spider webs and bats and trees in there. Here!" She began scrubbing again. I saw Fad's head rolling to either side, helpless. She stopped, reached around behind her and got the bowl. "Okay here, now spit out."

Wearing an exaggerated clown mouth of foam, Fad spat liquid into the bowl.

"I don't like you," he said, softly.

"And I don't like bacteria, darling. They want to hurt you. And nobody in the world can hurt my boy as long as his mother is brushing and flossing his mouth on a regular basis. Right?"

The floss. She grabbed it, unspooled a foot of it from its dispenser, wound it around her fingers, and leaned toward him, thumb and forefinger trussed with green filament.

"Stop!" cried Fad. "Mommy make me stop it!"

"In due time," said Harta soothingly.

THIRTEEN

The air grew hotter, then hotter still. I knew the sun was a planet of gas perpetually on fire in outer space, but it seemed impossible that *anything* happening 93 million miles away could make us feel this bad. When I asked Harta, she explained that this was not a heat wave, just the height of the summer, that it happened every year, and that every year I simply forgot it could get this hot. Weird bleachy patches appeared on parts of the lawn that Max had forgotten to water, and I saw several cars parked on the roads near our house with rigid hissing wands of steam above their radiators. People huddled under umbrellas in their bathing suits, misting themselves with garden hoses, or crept into their yards in the fading sunshine of dusk to trim their flower beds and mow their lawns. Often, on the very hot days, I wanted to go to the town pool, where the neat local kids spent their afternoons arm-wrestling, eating Fudgsicles, and even, I'd heard, smoking cigarettes together, but it was several miles away, and it was hard to get Harta to take me.

Instead, I stayed inside as much as possible, or lay in the rink of shade under the backyard willow tree. We had already gone to the shore and so there didn't seem much alternative to reading, watching the crash of the Yankees on television, reconnoitering the area around the house by telescope, and casually intercepting the mail and telephone calls while waiting for something to happen. Then, on July 21 it did. At 4 P.M. of that day, Harta picked up the phone and dialed a number. A moment later, she said, "Maude, you should know, I'm having a wonderful affair with a doctor—Herbert Minkoff." Listening on the downstairs extension, I slumped back against the basement wall, wanting simultaneously to cry, to point things out to the police, to go to Max with the certified news that a man, a living doctor, lay regularly atop my mother and rubbed inside her various mouths until she got flustered and red-faced and shouted (so I'd read) out loud. Instead of doing any of this, I did what I always did in situations of crashing helplessness and despair: I called Derwent.

"I want the doctor dead," I said.

"Yeah?" Derwent asked, and then, turning away from the phone, said in a slow, careful voice, "Do that once more, Mother, and I will kill you." Returning to the phone, he asked, "What's with the rancor, pal? The doc's big dick stinging your sneeze nerve? Oh, and by the way, I was going to tell you. We've got a name coming up from our statistical sweeps, one Herbert Demetrius Minkoff, M.D., a graduate in 1955 from, hang on"—there was a rustle of paper—"Tulane University."

"I know, Derwent. That's what I'm trying to tell you. My mom just blabbed it to her friend on the phone. It's as bad as we thought. She called it an *affair*."

"Heh-heh."

"I know we suspected it for weeks," I said, "but to find out for sure—I just can't believe she would do that."

"What?"

"*That*, to my dad. He's a decorated veteran. Did you know he was shot down in World War Two?"

Derwent snorted. "Maybe that explains his permanent bad mood. But hey, I don't care if he's General Dwight D. Eisenhoover. Stuff like this happens all the time. And remember: Parenthood is a sick joke anyway."

"How do you mean?"

"I mean it's unjust and it's wrong, buddy, not to mention inefficient. Two people you never even met before get drunk one night and ball—and that means you have to spend the next eighteen years walking around in hand-me-down pants, mumbling *bless this food our daily bread?* I mean, gimme a break! The fact is," Derwent went on, "there are certain children who are inexplicably born into families that are below them, and end up suffering horribly as a result. I'm just not going to let that happen to me. You know the story of Kaspar Hauser, I assume?"

"No."

"Neither do I." Derwent yawned loudly, and then said, "Speaking of parents, where are yours?"

"My parents? They just left to go shopping."

His teeth shut with a click. "Is he, uh, alone?"

"Affirmative."

"For more than an hour?"

"Definitely."

"I'll be right over," said Derwent, slamming down the phone.

Five minutes later he stood in the doorway, wearing tight black clam diggers, a stained T-shirt, and, on his face, the gigantic square sunglasses used by cataract patients.

"Snuff," he said, as he stepped inside. It was our new code, a private device of guy consensus. "Snuff," I answered, going over to look out the blinds, pretend interest in the details of cars and telephone poles, observe the occasional bird. We both knew what we were going to do, and yet we had to dice gently with it, give it some time to ripen. Cruelty is like that.

"Snuff," I heard from behind me.

We played it casual.

"What else have you been up to?" I asked.

"Nothing special." Derwent yawned, extended his arms in the air. "Ya know, chemistry 'n' shit. Dad bought a Dremel Moto-Tool to make model planes with. Needless to say, I'm putting it to a use Daddy-o never dreamed of."

"Oh yeah? What are you making?"

"A bazooka." Derwent smiled. "To bring down low-flying planes. The only problem is, I have a feeling my old man may actually be hep to the firearm."

"Why?"

"He's been real touchy with me lately, kind of weird actually, almost like he suspects something, the sneaky bastard."

I laughed. "Did you say weird?" I motioned upstairs. "He's in his room, alone."

"Snuff."

We crept up the stairs, cat-burglar-style, one after the other. In one of the bathrooms, we reconnoitered silently.

Derwent gestured to the medicine cabinet.

"Choose your weapons," he whispered.

I opened the door, skimmed my eyes over the Prell shampoo, the Tucks medicated pads, the strange plastic cases and yellowing prescription labels from doctors that seemed, somehow, to promise a future of agonizing pain and itching in still unknown body parts, and settled on a spray bottle of Aqua Net. Derwent, meanwhile, had reached under the sink for a bottle of Lemon Glade.

"Okay," I said, "fall out."

We walked toward Fad's room, hearing Trini Lopez music going quietly. The phone began to ring, but I ignored it. We crept farther down the hall, holding our lips in our teeth.

The door swung open with a catty yowl. The small room, its windows shut, had a deep personal smell. Fad was sitting on his bed, making his light cruising rock, little swoops and circles of movement.

"Hello Derwent," he said in his flat voice, and then smiled.

Fad didn't ever really know how to smile—which is probably why it intrigued me so. Harta had been working on the smile fairly heavily in the last couple of weeks, and she had, with time, managed a kind of strained upward-pointing curve to his features. It looked, truth be told, an awful lot like he had to shit, but that was all right by me.

"Hello, Fadley," said Derwent.

Fad's smile fell.

"That's not my name. My name is Fad, or James."

"A joke," said Derwent. "Forgive me, eccellenza. What-turya listening to?"

"Oh, music."

Fad stopped flicking and stood there.

Derwent and I exchanged a glance. The moment had arrived.

"Fad," I said, and came closer, "I have a special treat-ment Mommy said I was supposed to try on you."

"Ohhh," he said.

"It's very special," said Derwent, taking a step closer.

"Yes," said Fad, looking at me, and making his smile-grimace. "It's special. It's so special. How special is it?"

"Take your pants down."

"Sure." He unbuckled his pants, slid them down.

"Now your underwear," I said, taking a step closer.

"Right," he said, and pulled them down.

There it hung, a dimensional still life of pink grapes and tubers, framed in scraggly black hair. It looked, I thought, like a tiny old woman trying to suck her thumb.

I bent forward at the waist, putting my face up close.

"Yes, this is the one," I said, addressing it in a loud voice. I stood up, nodded my head soberly, and turned to Derwent.

"Dr. Blobstein? Your prognosis?"

Derwent came forward, bent over, and squinted.

"I was afraid of this," he said, standing up with a sigh. "It's an advanced case of Congo disorder, deep in the tertiary phase. The last person I saw with this is in a glass case in a museum somewhere. And the case," said Derwent sorrowfully, "is the size of a shoebox."

"That's right!" crowed Fad proudly.

"I'd recommend advanced fumigation," said Derwent.

"I'm afraid I'd have to agree," I added thoughtfully.

"Snuff," we said together, bending forward, bottles at the ready, and beginning to spray.

"Wheeee!" cried Fad, in a gush of happy air. "Yippeee!" he cried.

We stopped, stood up.

"See you later, jerk!" I cried, watching as Fad's face fell, and then continued to fall, and then drew right up again in a tightly knotted flower of pain.

"Owww it burns!" he screamed, as we went sprinting down the stairs and out into the grace of the sunset, drunk with joy.

The shock waves of the incident drifted slowly outward through the family, and for an entire day the topic was ignored. The next afternoon, Harta approached me where I sat perfectly upright in my room staring out the window. Concentrating hard, staring without blinking, I was trying, with my mind, to control a cloud.

"I've decided on a doctor for you," she said in a low voice.

"For me?" I turned from the cloud and looked at Harta.

"Yes." She forced a phony smile up the sides of her face. "I talked to Dr. Sobol on the phone recently, and he recommended a woman named Mrs. Danziger. I just spoke to her and she said she really wanted to meet you. She's a very interesting person—a therapist." This last word was pronounced with a kind of reverence.

"Hey, Ma, what's a Rorschach test?"

"A test with ink where you look at the shapes and explain them. Why do you—" She stopped in midsentence, looked closer, her fake sunniness gone. "How do you know about the Rorschach?" she asked slowly.

"Why does she want to meet me?" I asked, changing the subject.

"Oh, unh, she's . . ." I watched her struggling a moment, balancing between moods, unsure. "She's heard you're a very smart and interesting young man."

Ugh. I got up from the table, barely able to contain my fury. I hated Harta in her reflex optimistic mode. Didn't everyone see just how bogus her sunniness was?

"Where are you going?" she asked. Just barely, I kept from shouting, "To Dr. Minkoff, where you have affairs!" But I couldn't bring myself to—yet. Instead, I decided to go outside and kick the grass until I felt better.

FOURTEEN

Hating the adults around me was easy, because all of them were such obvious frauds. One afternoon when the heat let up I watched a garden party in the next-door backyard through our attic telescope, the men moving in short, straight lines around the trees and swing set, the women walking higher on their toes as they glided toward the picnic table, carrying trays of drinks and pretzels. The truth lay a few yards away from the sunny scene, in the nearby woods, where tubular sprinting animals with murder on their minds were getting ready to hunt, pin, and eat each other with their teeth. A gust of cheerful summer laughter flew up into the air. I pushed the telescope away and shut my eyes. I didn't have to look. I knew that under a nearby rock, slithering blind things, fused at the mouth, had just sucked the juice out of one another and died.

That was the truth, the truth of cruelty. And yet somehow, despite all the evidence to the contrary, people didn't know. Girls and women in the pastel shells of their dresses didn't know. Distracted fathers drinking whiskey in their studies at night didn't know. Especially mothers breathing clouds of cheerful phony words in your face didn't know. Only boys knew. They saw it everywhere they looked in life. Some participated, some didn't. But boys knew. They knew that cruelty would never disappoint them. They knew that acts of kindness only left you feeling kind, while cruelty provided instant membership in that most desirable thing of all: the club of men.

The door opened with a hiss. I got on. The elevator was like a little cage, lined with plush. I punched the button for the eleventh floor, and with an electric buzz, I rose, tiny angry numbers flashing me upward. The doors opened again and I walked to the end of the long hallway down a carpet that seemed covered with swirling, steamrollered butterflies and fruit. I was somewhere in New York City, having been driven there against my wishes that morning by Harta. I found number 11-F, per my instructions.

The door was ajar and I stepped inside.

I found myself in a large, dim apartment whose forking hallways were lined with cases of glass. In these cases, lit by pencil-thin beams from above, arrayed in waves upon waves before mirrors, was an enormous collection. Of what? Of everything, it seemed. Ivory carvings of elephants with drivers attached; splinters of wood whittled into likenesses of long-faced men; microscopically ribbed umbrellas and tiny HO-gauge shoes and socks and coats on bent wire figurines; a finger-sized marching band made entirely of walrus bristles; agates, pottery bits, striped seashells, and a series of books with writing in them too small to see.

I stared with my mouth open. Tininess was a paradise. It was a place to rest your mind. If something was small enough, it could end up being utterly ignored, out of the wind and away from eyesight. Staring, I felt these little objects reminding me of something in a book I'd recently read, the one about that crazy British sailor blown head over heels around the ocean into the adventure of his life. What was his name? Gulliver.

"Hello to you!" cried the therapist, Mrs. Danziger, bending down to me and extending a padded hand. "I welcome you to my apartment!"

She blazed greeting out of deep oval eyes, bright blue. Short and squat, she had the shape of a backyard snowman and a strange accent in her voice, a tone of foreignness that somehow suggested overcast skies, border guards, and the waving fingers of searchlights in the night. Harta had explained that she was Polish, and had "suffered like nobody's business in the war." Her breath was tart.

I nodded, smiling narrowly, and followed her into another room, a roundish space at whose center was a low wooden table with two soft chairs on either side, and bowls of pretzel sticks and M&Ms in its center. Across the air shaft, in another apartment, a potbellied guy in an undershirt was sitting in his own window, staring up into the sky.

What was he looking at?

Mrs. Danziger motioned to a chair with small stirring movements of her fingertips. Obediently, I sat. She templed her hands together and rested her chin on them, pulling her face up in a smile that revealed tiny square teeth, like nibblets of baby corn, and cheerful fans of wrinkles at the corners of her eyes.

I smiled back. Distantly I heard a police siren begin. A long moment passed during which the siren rose, flared once, dwindled speedily to silence.

"Are you feeling well?" she asked.

"Oh yeah."

"Happy at home this summer?"

"Sure."

"Your mother tells me you like science."

"I do."

She reached a hand out, grabbed a pretzel, nibbled at it.

"I also heard this is a big summer for your family."

Was she waiting for me to comment? I said nothing.

"Lots of things going on?"

Again I said nothing.

She sighed, leaned back in the chair. Her bosom jutted.

"Tell me about your brother."

"My brother?" Not, I thought, again.

"What's the first thing you think about when you think about him?"

Disgusted, I thought. He was tall, goofy, et cetera. He screamed out loud in the public world. He had a big dick, curly hair, tiny scabbed spicules on his lips from biting himself. His lashes were long.

"Nothing."

Mrs. Danziger smiled, templed her fingers together.

"Nothing at all?" she said patiently. "Surely there must be something about him that comes to mind."

I looked down at the little domed piles of M&Ms and pretzel sticks. Grabbing some of each, I stuffed my mouth full of crackling sweet-sourishness.

"Nah."

Then, silence again, a long, deep silence. Suddenly I heard her say, "Let's play."

"What?"

She reached under the table and brought out a little box. I recognized it: pick-up sticks.

"So, and here is what we do."

She tilted the box onto the table. With a clatter, a stream of plastic needles poured out and into a rickety pile.

"Do you know the rules?" she asked.

"All the way," I said, using one of Derwent's favorite expressions.

Mrs. Danziger smiled, and extended a hand. On this hand, the exact tan color of rain blotting on the concrete of sidewalks, was an array of liver spots, linked by veins. I watched the hand, in a light trance. It silently withdrew a green stick. I reached forward, snatched one myself.

"Very good," she said. "I can tell I'm up against an expert."

Dusk outside the window began to deepen, seemingly from the ground up. I lifted my eyes and saw the man in the undershirt. Having finished his TV dinner, he was staring calmly out into the darkening evening. For some reason, suddenly, I was furious at him. I was getting ready to draw up a formal indictment in my mind, Perry Mason–style, when it occurred to me that Mrs. Danziger had already moved.

"What are you staring at so fiercely?" she asked.

"Nothing."

She spun her head around rapidly and stared at the man a moment.

"Does he remind you of someone?"

"No."

She smiled mysteriously again, and we resumed playing. The idea of the game was something like eating a chicken, I realized. You chewed away all the meat and were finally left with the truth of the bones. Bit by bit we picked away at the carcass, and as we played, Mrs. Danziger continued to move her voice gently around the inside of my head.

"I bet your brother would be good at this," she said, nodding at the pointy scatter on the table.

Instead of answering, I concentrated on the removal of

a central supporting needle—a part that, in a log cabin, I had recently learned, was called the *ridgepole*.

"Or one of your good friends," she said.

I looked up at her. She was smiling at me brightly.

"What?" I asked. "My friends? Like which friends?"

"Oh," she said, and grabbed her lower lip in her square little teeth and lightly, easily plucked another needle from the pile. "That would be for you to tell me." She tapped the withdrawn plastic needle against the pads of her fingers. "Any friends in particular come to mind?"

Perhaps I wanted to boast. I suddenly said, "Well, I sometimes spend time with a boy named Derwent. He's two years older than me, but he seems like a grownup."

"Why is that?"

"I don't know. I guess because he's so smart. He's the smartest person I know."

"What kinds of things do you two do together?"

"Oh, you know, we play games. We play catch sometimes. We have dirt-bomb fights." There was a pause. Spontaneously, I said, "We plan."

"You what?"

"We plan things—to do things, funny things."

I was unsure what I was saying. There was a feeling of crumbling in my stomach. I moved my feet together nervously.

"I see. You plan things."

I grabbed a huge fistful of pretzel sticks, jammed the clot of them in my mouth. Unable to speak, but chomping busily, I looked at her.

"Tell me more," said the bosomy weird Mrs. Danziger.

Swallowing, I said, "I'm not sure I can."

"Why?"

"Well, we—um we promised to keep things secret, you see."

"Ah, you made a pact?"

"Yeah," I jumped gratefully on the word. "A pact, like blood brothers."

"And what was the nature of this pact?"

"That we would never tell on one another."

"And," she continued in her calm, relentless way, "are there things in particular about which you should never tell?"

"I think there are."

"And do these things have to do with your family?"

"Maybe."

"I see."

She stopped leaning forward and seemed suddenly to relax. Mrs. Danziger folded her hands just below her chin, a gesture that gave her the appearance of a bird of some sort—an owl.

"I think it is important that we get to know one another better, Denny. And the way people do that is they tell the truth to one another. Your mother sent you to see me not only to play pick-up sticks and admire my collection of souvenirs, but because she was concerned about you. And so, actually, am I."

"You are?" I was surprised. "What did I do?"

"You didn't *do* anything," she said, and smiled. "It was what was done to you. But my point is I want you to feel comfortable talking about the way you feel, with me, here, today. Okay?"

I said nothing, merely sat there feeling sluggish, inert.

"Now aside from Derwent, who else is there?"

"I have lots of friends," I said, the pleasure all gone suddenly from my words. I was angry at Harta for having set me up with this prying person. I was furious at not being able to counter a weird slippage she induced in my self-control. Therefore, I said as little as possible, and answered her in crimped little words for the next half hour. When our time was finally over and she was saying good-bye, I observed, to my happiness, a certain tightness in the bracketing wrinkles on her forehead and around her mouth. Going down in the ancient elevator I began whistling—the first few bars of "Old MacDonald Had a Farm," repeated over and over again.

Harta was waiting for me on the street below in her turret-shaped Corvair, its motor idling like a dry cough, windows jammed shut even though the air was scorching. "Animals," Harta had said of New Yorkers to me, "who will claw the life out of your body for a crust of bread." I looked in the car window. She was reading a book called *The Autobiography of Lincoln Steffens* and eating chocolate nonpareils from a box in her lap. Fad lay on his side in the backseat, asleep with his mouth open and his hands between his knees. I tapped on the window and she glanced up with a fearful look before her face broadened into a wide smile.

"How'd it go, sweet?" she asked, flinging open the door.

"I don't want to talk about it," I said, getting in. The car was cool from the air-conditioning, which had a chemical odor. Fad was blinking groggily.

"I can't tell you," Harta said, pulling the snorting car into traffic, "just how proud you've made me."

Dinner that night was Harta's special beef Stroganoff, made with "a special lean meat" that she'd convinced the butcher to give her "with a fabulous bribe." Winking wildly at me, she tried to ladle extra portions of the steamy, runny food on my plate, but I wasn't interested. I felt enormously tired, went to bed early, fell instantly asleep, and that night, for the very first time, I dreamed of Death. A gaunt black figure entered the field of my sleeping vision, and in greeting, raised a star-shaped puff of smoke. There was an end to living after all, the figure explained in a calm voice, and this was called

Death. The words stopped. The body ended. It was like reading a book that erased itself as you went along, and when you
finished there was a heap of dust and powdery bones on the
floor where before there had been sentences slung like bright
webbing above the world and the story of a life filled with
beautiful, slow-moving men and women. Death might come as
a pair of gleaming black bookends, fashioned of the pure cold
of outer space, that squeezed your head from either side until
you exploded in a single breath-shaped burst, and went away.
Or maybe it was a hole in the world, through which you passed
like a gas, and from which you never, absolutely ever, came
back.

I sat up in bed with a jerk, my heart pounding. It was
night, the house was quiet. There was a familiar snoring sound
from the bedroom next to mine, faintly audible through the
closet door. No, Fad's extinction I wouldn't have especially
mourned, just then. But the thought that my parents, in all
their vividness, voices, and big bodies, would one day simply
be hooked off the planet and dumped, somewhat like weeds,
in holes in the earth, sickened me.

The cosmos to my understanding was a comfy place,
swirly with stars at night, and by day filled with the puffy
unreal shapes of clouds over which some force, some thing
with a face nearly human, brooded steadily, doling out the
good and the bad. Clearly, if any family was good, it was ours
with its music and books and painstaking concern for justice
in the world. Surely, in such a scheme of things, there would
be room for a small oversight, for a tiny slipup, a rent in the
membrane through which my parents, miraculously, might
squeeze?

FIFTEEN

The only escape out of things seemed to be to get sick. To get red, rashy, weak in the head; to feel yourself shooting up tall, and then suddenly shrinking, or to experience the sensation that your skin had been drawn taut like the top of a tom-tom drum, and made to throb. Temporary sickness could be inhaled from the poisonous particles brewing in the air over the smoky town dump, which would turn your face dependably green for two days; it could be gulped from certain of the potions with which Harta caused her body to smell like a garden (Prince Matchabelli worked like a charm). Sickness was rest; sickness was attention; sickness, above all, was a way to swing the focus of the family away from Fad.

Another more specific advantage to being sick was that it allowed me to watch Vietnam on television without interruption and for hours at a time. When baseball wasn't on that summer, there was always Vietnam—a loop of hilly green forests, little men with skewed Asian eyes, and peaceful villages erupting in flame. On top of Vietnam, there was that other war, the war that was taking place on the streets of America right under our noses and in living color. This was the war waged by students against the war in Vietnam, who could be seen on television in broad daylight shouting, running, and falling as if in combat. They carried signs and peace symbols and were trampled regularly by the horses of the police. Blood gushed through their long hair and down their colorful T-shirts. If they were boy students, they sometimes fought openly with the police, throwing punches like on real boxing matches.

The television came on in an explosion of spindling lines. These resolved into young men with their mouths open. They were firing heavy machine guns. It was the battle of the American airbase at Da Nang. I was sick again, with a rare summer sore throat. I watched American black men with rags on their heads pulling white men to safety through the searing yellow flowers of exploding bombs. In the cities of America, black people were just then having "a long, hot" summer, which meant that they were burning down buildings and looting stores in their unhappiness. This was yet another war, though commentators spoke of it as a kind of giant disease, a "virus of unrest" that spread from one city to another in a chain of contaminations. On the television, the different wars revolved in a smooth, confusing, eye-level band—black men sprayed with police hoses, set upon by dogs and clubbed to the ground, and then rising upward again as green-suited soldiers holding stuttering machine guns aimed at the enemy "in defense of liberty." Every few minutes, the camera spun away from the various wars to a press conference, where American military men whirled and stabbed at their maps, while sending up what Max had explained were great, wordy clouds of lies. The Vietnam War was lies from beginning to end, with one catch: It was being fought with real people. None of this stopped me in the least from enjoying the spectacle, and particularly napalm, which fell from American fighter planes and hit the

ground in great tumbling, forward-moving streaks of fire, like
a pianist striking his fingers into the keys.

"C'mon, sweetie, drink your broth," said Harta. I made
a face, wished her out of the room. Through a slight ringing
in my ears I listened to Morley Safer speaking over the sound
of sniper fire. He was declaring that the Vietcong, against all
odds, were advancing. They were nearby, he said. His voice
shook. For heaven's sake, he cried, let's get a move on and
close this report! The bullets crackled around him like applause, while shells whistled then thumped and the earth
jumped out of itself with great enthusiasm.

The television image dwindled to a dot, grew right back
up to Walter Cronkite speaking from the calm of a studio. His
face was covered all over with honest lines, and he seemed to
be willing himself to talk slowly and deliberately.

"Never since World War Two has there been an American intervention on this massive a scale," said Walter
gravely. I spooned broth, electrified at the thought of a massive
intervention. "The president has placed nearly four hundred
thousand troops in Vietnam, fighting to defend American in-
terests."

Later that same night, I woke up out of a sound sleep
in the darkness and thought: It's begun. Vietcong are sliding down ropes into the chimneys of America, bayoneting
babies, and tearing our flag to bits with their yellow teeth.
But no: It was something else, an entirely new category of
angry sounds. The noises were harsh, specific, and strangely
varied, too, as if someone were chiming the contents of a
bedroom with a stick—bedposts, dresser, vases, and windows hit and sounding out in turn. As my head cleared, I
realized that what I was hearing were the voices of my parents, but voices raised to a pitch of fury, voices punching
holes in the air at high speed. I couldn't distinguish words,

just the violent collisions of sounds. And then, as I listened, there was suddenly a smash like a bomb going off. This was followed by Max and Harta screaming again, at an even higher pitch. Too frightened to move, I lay still and sent a single finger riffling backward through the files of my mind. I was attempting to be "orderly and direct in thought" per the instructions on desert survival in my British RAF manual, and the four relevant facts I drew out and looked at as my parents clubbed each other with their voices were these: One, as the summer had gone on Harta had only grown more obsessed with Fad; she was now talking to him nearly constantly about the way he looked, and praising him with her fake flutey voice, touching him here and there with quick little jabs of the thumb, smudging something off his lip, or flipping his hair off his forehead. Two, she was wearing lots of makeup, moving around the house looking like an oil painting of herself, and spending increasingly long afternoons "out." Three, Max was miserable, silent and slit-eyed, drinking more and more and with that bitter yeasty odor of alcohol around him every evening upon his return from work. The question that gnawed at me constantly was, Did Max know? Was he aware of what his wife, my mother with the piled hair, was doing with her afternoons? And most importantly, did the house feel the way it did because Max knew, or because he didn't?

"Dad," I asked him the next day, "do you know?"

"Know what, Denny?" Max said, his smile of hello fading on his face. He was just home from work and standing in my doorway in his boxy blue suit. I looked at his face, and at the colors of eyes, hair, and lips arrayed like living bits on the wheel of a target. Uncertain where to shoot my glance, I aimed it over his head.

"Do you know what Mom does with her afternoons?" I asked a far corner.

"Mom, huh?" Max drew his hands down his lips, as if smoothing an invisible mustache. "Well I guess you'd be the expert there, wouldn't you, Denny?"

I sat up in bed. "I'll tell you, Dad. Mom goes to a matinee movie with Maude on Monday. On Wednesday she sees Jackie Kagan for lunch, and they go to the Great Wall of China on Route Twenty-three. Mom usually has the pu-pu platter, and Jackie has the egg foo young."

Max, holding half his face very serious, let the other half drift upward, as if amused.

"Off the top of my head, I'd say you've got a hell of a lot of spare time on your hands, sonny. How do you know about all this stuff anyway?"

"I just listen to what Mom says," I said, omitting that the listening took place almost exclusively over the telephone.

"You just listen . . . ," Max repeated again, and then, still staring at me, bit his lip.

"Son, stay here for just a second, will ya?"

"Sure."

He went out of the room. I had a pretty good hunch what he was doing. Sure enough, when he came back to me a moment later, he had that look on him, that wide open blinking look I recognized. Max leaned against the wall, crossed his arms on his chest, and faced me.

"Okay, son. Here's your big chance to tell me who else your mother goes to see in the afternoons, since you seem to have such a perfect knowledge of her social schedule."

"Well." I cleared my throat just like Derwent. "According to my records, Mommy sometimes goes to have tea and sponge cake with Mrs. Reiner, from West Caldwell. That's usually on Thursday. Twice a week she attends a class in learning trends for the disabled at the Orange Community Center, and on Mondays she browses at Korvettes and Two Guys. Sometimes she goes to the Home department of Alexander's to look for silverware and place settings."

"Unbelievable," Max said to himself, under his breath. "Frigging unbelievable. And what else?"

I was waiting for my chance. "There are several other people she sees on a regular basis."

Max leaned forward slightly.

"Who would they be?"

"She goes to a health club where a woman named Trina massages her every week."

"Yes? And?"

"And . . . uh." I felt a name slide heavily off a shelf inside my mind, and fall all the way to the bottom, *thump!*

"And what, son?"

"And I guess that's it." I slumped, deflated.

"Well!" he said, clapping his hands together to change the subject. "That's enough spywork for a day in any case." He gave me a wink. "Let's worry a little less about state secrets and more about getting well and up and about in a few days, eh? Now drink your broth and get some rest, okay?"

"Sure thing, Dad."

SIXTEEN

A s soon as I was well again, I phoned Sabina. It seemed important to reconnect with the clean, calm air I always felt around her—especially after four clammy days in bed and the recent late-night explosion at our house. I relished the thought of spending time around the person whom Harta, in a weird voice, had recently described as "a living doll." When I called, Sabina greeted me on the phone with her usual cheerful voice, and said she'd been thinking about me, and did I want to come over? A half hour later, I was sitting in front of her in her bedroom, a place furnished, it seemed to me, so as to provide the experience of living in a cloud. Pink cloths dripped off the dresser, purled across the floor; rose fabric extended in a canopy atop the four-poster bed. Even the sunlight seemed tinted, cute, and deferential.

"He's dead," she said, looking sorrowfully into the distance.

"Who?" I asked.

"Ferdinand."

Too upset to speak, she gestured to a small wooden frame. In it was a photograph of a hamster—an animal I vaguely remembered as a silly little piece of fur that sat in a corner of their garage and stared at you with button eyes.

"No one understood the deep, true feelings he had," she said softly. "I used to read books to him. I sang songs. He loved to sit and listen. His favorite book was *The Little Prince.*"

"*The Little Prince,*" I repeated, confused.

"He was a beautiful soul. And he was against the war, too."

I *had* to change the subject. I said, "My parents had a big fight."

"Really?"

"Yeah, I thought they were going to kill each other, Sabina. It was kinda neat, but scary, too."

Sabina looked at me and then blew her nose with a dainty honk. "The problem with you," she said, folding her handkerchief into little squares, "is that you suspect the worst of everybody, your parents included. Don't you realize that people are mostly good in life? Otherwise, what would the point be, right?"

"I guess," I said, uncertain.

"I want to save you," said Sabina, "save you in the name of Christ our lord. Once you're saved, you can relax and enjoy an eternity of Christian happiness. And eternity is so beautiful, Denny, like an endless sunny day. In the meantime, would you do me a favor?"

"What's that?"

"Would you stay away from Derwent Prine?"

Sabina, in her perfect room, stood up and began to pace.

"Look, it's not just that I don't like him. There are many people I don't like. I think he's genuinely dangerous. I can see the man growing up into Lee Harvey Oswald. Please, Denny, please promise me you won't see him again?"

I laughed, despite her seriousness. Somewhere up on one of my shelves was the Warren Commission report on the Kennedy assassination—a black buckram-covered volume the size and density of a small phone book. I'd read nearly every page, breathless for details of bullet flight paths and airborne presidential brain matter.

"Don't worry about it," I said confidently. "I've got the guy eating out of my pocket."

She stopped pacing. "I think you mean eating out of your hand, don't you?"

"I suppose I do, yeah."

"Anyway," she said, resuming her walking, "what do you see in him?"

"His mind, mainly. Derwent's a genius." I loved that word. It seemed so robust and categorical and made everything so simple.

"Maybe he is a genius, but who cares? You're too easily impressed, Denny." She frowned. "Derwent Prine has a heart the size of a chicken liver."

"You really think so?" I asked, my mind involuntarily falling back to the summer before, when myself, Greg Mancuso, and Terry Daley, paid in advance by Derwent, together caught Connie Clearfall on a far green corner of the playing field where she was walking her poodle, and pinioned her to the grass. A small rise concealed our workings from the rest of the world. Derwent had pursued Connie for a kiss all year long in school and been rejected, sometimes angrily. Now he had Connie caught, writhing in explosions of long hair, and making horsey faces of distress while shrieking with fancy expressions she had learned from the movies. Holding a limb, I bent close, amazed at the translucency of her skin, its fine, glowing coat of whiteness. She was flinging her head from side to side, throwing her limbs about. "Unhand me!" she screamed. "Help, police!" she cried.

Derwent hit her square on the face with the flat of his hand, and she went absolutely still. Without any advance warning, she relapsed quietly in the dirt. As if for the very first time, horrified, I stared at what we'd done. She now lay broken and quiet in our hands. Her yellow plaid jumper was infused with tea-colored stains of lawn. Her white blouse had mud on the elbows. Mingling with the eyeliner she wore, her tears had described skinny, long-tailed blots upon her skin, like sperm. Looking at this small, pale, tear-stained face, I thought that she was the most perfect human being I'd ever seen.

"I want her pubes!" screamed Derwent, considerably, at the moment, out of his mind. The three of us boys stared a moment at each other. Then, as one, we jumped him. Letting her go, we grabbed him, punched him, beat him wildly about the face and chest, and hauled him off of her where he lay throbbing and bucking in pain on his side. Greg Mancuso, with a running start, went up to him and kicked him right in the balls.

"I don't think he's violent at all," I said, looking Sabina steadily in the eye.

She shook her head in disappointment. "You're just a friend to me," she said, "not a boyfriend or anything. But even as a friend . . . I wish you'd stop seeing that jerky person."

"I'll think about it," I said. Eager to change the subject, I got up and walked over to a large glass case of dolls set along one wall.

"Dolls," I said, peering close, fascinated.

"Yes," said Sabina, and stood a moment, as if deciding whether or not to close the topic of Derwent. Her shoulders slumped: She was done. She came forward, her face lightening.

"Most of these dolls are of bisque porcelain," she said in her lecturer's voice, leaning over and sliding open the glass doors of the cabinet. "They were imported by the thousands from Germany and France at the beginning of the century as toys for the children of rich people. Here." She removed a doll and with great care placed it in my arms.

I stared at the thing. Its body was as cold as death, and its snubbed and shiny face, eyes closed, seemed lifeless.

"Notice the painting of the hair, and the perfect whiteness of the bisque enamel," she said. "This is a Jumeau doll, which is one of the rarest, most valued of companies. Rock it."

"What?"

"Rock it, as if it were a baby girl you wanted to put to sleep."

"No, I don't think so."

"Denny, please, don't be a silly. Rock it."

I rocked. As if on cue, its little eyes flew open. At the back of my head, I felt a cold-watery tightening.

"These are what are called 'sleep eyes,'" she said, "to give the impression of an awakening child."

"Huh," I said, giving the doll back to her, and reaching down to where a shinier little face awaited. This was a Chatty Cathy doll, a creature the mystery of whose drawling mechanical voice had lodged itself in my head several years before and stuck there. How did it make that sound? I picked it up. Sabina seemed embarrassed.

"Something a nurse gave me," she said, angling her eyes downward. "Who knows, maybe I'll give it to the Salvation Army."

On impulse, I asked, "Can I have it?"

"What, the Chatty Cathy? But why, Denny? It's such a silly thing."

I pulled the string. Immediately the dwarf scratchy voice sang out, "Hello, I'm Chatty Cathy, what's your name?"

It sounded as if it were arriving through a bathtub of standing water.

"I just like it is all," I said, concealing my excitement.

Sabina stared, attempted to size me up, and then threw her hands up in a little gesture of compliance.

"Sure, okay, if you want it." We chatted a few more minutes, and as soon as I was able, I detached myself from her, and rushed home holding the large doll down one leg, a posture that seemed as inconspicuous as possible. My route lay across the grassy backyards of several homes, and included a speedy shortcut across the Sullivans' rear patio. I was in love with shortcuts, and had been so ever since Derwent explained to me that the more of them one took in life, the longer one lived. He claimed to have the formula explaining this somewhere in his files.

I got to our front lawn, hobbling furiously with the doll, whose eyes were wide open and whose face, flush against my denimed leg, was fixed in a deep and bitterly determined smile. Opening the screen door, I barreled fast into the main hallway of the house, took a quick visual check to ensure no one saw me, and then rushed down the stairs to the basement, where I was swallowed up in the cool quiet.

This was Max's lair—a dad's world. His workshop, usually locked, was open for once, and I walked inside. The air was uniformly gray. Spills of brightly insulated wire poured from the various shelves in plastic cataracts. Large, toothed and cogged instruments stood still. The industrial spices in the air signaled to me that world of high purpose, body hair, and heavy machinery that seemed inhabited exclusively by fathers.

I lay the Chatty Cathy doll down on the workbench. The doll's brittle golden hair expanded in shining waterfalls on either side of its head, lips parted as if in light breathing. I looked closer. Her hair was salted onto her head through a grid of tiny holes. I had struck my first disappointment: There were holes in her head!

Chatty Cathy was dressed in a brown woolen frock that Sabina or her mother had probably sewn for her. Carefully unbuttoning it, I took it off. Below that was a slip of some kind. That came off quickly.

Cathy, as I now referred to her, was naked. Lying facedown, her ass was high, full, and deeply cloven. She was painted a foul pasty color that was utterly fake.

Hoping for the best, I flipped her back over again, and pretending to look elsewhere, scanned her crotch. It was smooth, square, and without detail. I touched her there, but only for a second, and then turned her back over again.

Pulling the string brought with it the same imbecile rote "Hello, I'm Chatty Cathy, what's your name?" The voice seemed sucked in as much as spoken. I observed that it came from a small grilled speaker in the doll's neck.

We would see about this Chatty Cathy.

Going to the toolbox, I withdrew a nasty-looking ball peen hammer, and then stood staring into space a moment. The first blow came crashing through at the doll's throat, leaving a nasty gaping wound and the sharp stink of styrene in the air. I picked up Cathy, trembling slightly with excitement, and peered inside. A couple of wires, no surprise there, but there was nothing else I could see.

The next cracking blow caved in a piece of Chatty Cathy's sternum. Another demolished her solar plexus. Now there were big broken plates of pinkish doll flesh lying on the workbench. Cathy's serene expression was unchanged, but her body was in pieces.

There it was. My *prize*. Deep within the innards of her body was a chrome box, and when I turned it over, on the other side was a tiny record player—tone arm, spindle, and the lustrous black disk—tiny, so tiny I was in awe.

Sweeping the pieces into a paper bag, I hesitated long and hard over the head. It continued to stare stubbornly, serenely. I held it up, feeling its hollowness, smelled it, and thought a moment about what to do next.

Attached to Max's workbench was an enormous vise. I placed the doll head in the vise and began closing it. I then continued to close it, cranking hard, until, with a loud, satisfying crack, the doll head broke in half.

AUGUST

SEVENTEEN

As the summer finally peaked, seeming to lengthen into an endless hallway of sunshine, slow motion, and thick air, a thought arrived, setting down in the center of my mind like a butterfly. The thought was this: that every girl I knew had a living body, forked and tufted in its middle, which she took to bed with her, washed in the morning, and put food into three times a day. Up till that moment I had admired girls with the same respectful feelings I had for the Constitution, Democracy, or the Rights of Man. They were not to be touched, but merely glanced at and sat next to, talked with and made to laugh whenever possible. I had no sister, and perhaps because of that especially loved the way their faces looked when hit horizontally by rays of light: how easily they assumed the curved, simple shapes of the letters in the handwriting exercises we did in school, or batted their eyelashes and ran with boylike power straight across a field of grass. I enjoyed the way they so effortlessly discussed things, filling like a sail with excitement and gossip and then turning with no warning into complete seriousness.

And now, bodies. Under skirts and dresses, bodies. Beneath the makeup, the crispness of voices raised to answer questions in class, the hair falling on either side of the face like the covers of an upside-down book, bodies.

No hair had yet leafed from *my* crotch. No thick pads of muscle had yet swelled *my* sticklike arms and legs. But Derwent, earlier that summer, had pulled me aside one afternoon and proudly shown me his wisps of pubic beard, and I had also noticed among certain of my larger friends that the cornsilk covering our legs and arms had already begun to be replaced by something more coarse and manly. Growing up, it was clear, was going to be yet another kind of race—a race toward size and height, booming voices, and the incredible speed and power of being a man. Already I was filling with the beginnings of something. It was merely the barest thickening of parts of skin, a certain drawing feeling around the roots of hair. But I had suddenly begun to understand its power, felt its wind ripple across my flesh at the beginning of that August.

I put aside Doc Savage. I slid Tom Swift and Jules Verne back into their spaces on the shelf. The book I was suddenly interested in was called *Van de Velde's Guide to Marriage,* an old, cigar-smelling volume I'd seen on a high shelf in Max and Harta's bedroom. As soon as I had a chance, I retrieved it, and later that same night, dinner over, opened it and eagerly began to read. The pages were full of diagrams and arrows, lengthy descriptions, and aromatic foreign words: *labia minora, urethra, clitoris.* Reading, I felt the wind again, a faintest whisper. And then, suddenly, without warning that wind began to blow. It was as if a hundred small veins had suddenly decided to wring themselves together and empty into a larger stream. Locks unlocking, bolts shooting open in greased tracks—something within me backed off, and then rushed forward in hot, pulsating specificity.

Did I have to pee? I furled back the sheet and looked

down expectantly. Craning mutely, blind but excited, the center of my body was swimming out on the air, seeming very determined that it get somewhere, and fast.

There was a loud knock.

"Who is it?"

"Mommy."

It was bedtime and she wanted to rub my back, of course. She wanted to draw her fingers along the wings of my back—scapulae, Derwent had explained they were called when I'd told him about it.

"Just a minute," I said frantically, praying for the outflow of blood and remembering Derwent. "Jeez, she does that?" he'd asked, concerned, when I told him about our nightly back rubs.

"Yeah."

"Has she ever tried to cop a feel?"

"What?"

"Your mom, does she touch you?"

I must have a made a threatening face, because he raised his hands and took a step back.

"Hey, don't get huffy. Lots of moms do. Mine, wouldn't you know, is too uptight to consider it. But Craig Bluff is doing it with his. So is Vinnie Malfitano and Frank Rhodes." He leaned forward and said in a low voice, "Randy Galbraith says his mom blows him every other night."

Harta knocked louder at the door, asking, "Don't you want me to come in, darling?"

I looked down into my lap, at the bud of flesh there, rigid and furious. I felt suddenly dizzy.

"Uh, Ma, I think I'm okay tonight alone."

"Are you sure?" She twisted the knob—but fruitlessly. I had locked it.

"Yes, I'm fine."

"Listen," she said in a new no-nonsense tone of voice. "I'd just like to check on you, please."

"No, Mom, that's okay. I'm really fine, really."

"Are you absolutely, positively sure?"

"Yes." -

There was a pause. And then, trailing waves of hurt silence, Harta withdrew. I looked down. A minute earlier my willy had been waving at the world like a student with the right answer, but to my disappointment, it was now listing perilously to one side, nodding silently off to sleep.

The next day, I woke up eager to know more about the wind. After completing a morning round of light note-taking in which I indexed Harta's phone calls (Maude, Dr. Haselfritz, and Dr. Stern) and the subject of that day's home lessons with Fad (Shirt Buttoning, Shoe Tying, and Posture), I strolled down the hill toward Derwent's, determined to find out what he knew. When no one answered my knock, I let myself in, and followed a low buzzy roar of voices to the basement, where I found Derwent lying alone on an old busted green couch, watching *McHale's Navy* on TV. I looked around. Webby, icky stuff dripped off the furniture. A kind of blue-cheese mottling had eaten upward along the legs of the couch. Even the air seemed drained.

"Derwent," I said.

He raised a right hand in a vaguely papal gesture of welcome as I went over and sat down next to him on the couch, a move that raised a spray of ancient dust. As the dust settled, I began setting out my questions about the new wind I'd begun to feel in my nerves—origins, duration, intensity. But I soon stopped. It was clear that Derwent wasn't listening. His gaze, instead, was riveted on the small television across the room. I glanced over and saw a shimmering snowfield of static, behind which, vaguely, I could make out a PT boat cruising silently across a lagoon. The boat docked. A commercial came on—shouting voices of tiny people in someone's sink. Derwent turned to me.

"I listened to only one word in three you were just saying," he said.

"How's that?" I asked.

"It's a new technique I learned to cut down on mental fatigue. And even listening to only a third of it, I want to tell you: Big deal."

"What do you mean?" I said indignantly.

"About your big new discovery. The *wind*. What're you, a poet? So you popped a rod. Don't get all goopy about it."

Before I could say anything, Derwent added, "We have only forty-nine seconds left to this commercial, so I'm going to get to the point fast."

"What's the point, Derwent?"

"The point is, squirt, that if you're really serious about this wind in your pants you'll sit here and wait while I get something ready."

"What something?"

"Wait and see. In the meantime, if you want"—he gestured to a dark corner of the room—"you can play some records."

As he went upstairs, I wandered over to the hi-fi, which was an old Magnavox with controls collared with filth and a turntable that stacked records like flapjacks. I cued up *Purple Haze* by Jimi Hendrix and put on the headphones.

When the song began, I settled back in a chair and began daydreaming. The music helped, revolving a wheel of images in front of my closed eyes: Harta and her soft voice and big body and the penciled curves of her face; her wedding invitation lying up in the attic, gathering dust but with the lettering raised on it like the veins of a hand: *Mr. and Mrs.*

Mirrow proudly announce the engagement of their daughter; I saw a hose spray once, violently, then twice Max's face drifted into view, contorted as if digesting something of great bitterness, the pink hoop of his mouth opening and closing in slow words. And I thought of the wind, blowing everywhere over the planet, a force of terrible power and hunger raising itself like a fist to strike inside a billion bodies. As the band of pictures spun fast, then faster, the images began to appear elongated from sheer speed: There was Sabina and several of her friends, faces pulled sideways from the spinning, whirling velocity, their hair stiff in the breeze. Faster and faster still spun the wheel, as the music roared and the wind roared, too, and then like a plane taxiing down the runway, an enormous heaviness suddenly became light, light as air, light as ease in the sunshine.

"I bet you look like that when you come."

I opened my eyes. The music had stopped. Derwent was standing in front of me, speaking into a microphone attached to the stereo. I blinked, disoriented.

"You have that kind of ooky look on your face."

"What?" My mouth had been open and I shut it with a click.

"Like the Mona Lisa giving a blow job," said Derwent, who extended a long knobby finger in the air and crooked it. "Follow me."

"You asshole." I was deeply embarrassed.

Derwent laughed.

"God, I love Jimi Hendrix," he said, pointing up the stairs.

I followed him to his brother Robbie's room, where an explosion of diagrams and old-style illustrations seemed to have flung its contents all over the place. The walls were literally upholstered with paper cutouts of microscopes and scales and glassware from scientific supply catalogs, taped, stapled, and pasted into place. Plus, there was magician's paraphernalia everywhere, including a blazing portrait of "Cardini" done in oils, a top hat, gloves, and funny yellowing advertisements for magic tricks from the 1930s with titles like "The Egg Bag" and "The Swimming Rings." The air smelled bad. Robbie, I remembered, was ugly just like Derwent, but skinnier, ganglier, more lyrically unattractive. I took it all in, and then noticed that at the foot of his brother's bed there was an electric fan, with the sheet of the bed taped around its cowling.

"Ladies and gentlemen," said Derwent, giving his words a flourish, "I'd like you to meet the world's very first hand-tested and deep-down-guaranteed-to-please Tunnel of Love."

"Tunnel? What tunnel?"

"This very tunnel here," said Derwent, and going to the wall, he flicked on a switch. The fan zoomed, and the top sheet of the bed slowly inflated and then hung there, engorged. He had created a kind of cocoon, or tunnel.

"Ha," I said, "that's pretty cool. What's it for?"

"I've decided you need help," he said.

"Yeah, what kind of help?"

"Help in learning how better to do it."

"What?"

"Come on. You know." He jigged a fist up and down. "Frig, dad. Scootchy-koo. You get inside this thing, and it's like being held in the arms of a movie star—but hey, get with it, it's a jerk-off tunnel."

A jerk-off tunnel? My face took on a frown. "No thanks," I said to Derwent, whose mouth fell open in astonishment. "What do you mean, no thanks?" he said. "We're talking the latest top-of-the-line whack-off technology, and you're telling me you're not interested? Hey, wait!" I was walking down the stairs of his house. It seemed important to get away. "Hey, asshole! You fucking fairy! Hey wait a second." His voice grew fainter as I walked out his front door and moved swiftly up the hill, thinking to myself, The *wind* is pure; the *wind* is clean; the *wind* doesn't have long stringy hair and yellow spots on its teeth, or touch itself with a fist, giggling.

"Dr. Minkoff is your dad!" Derwent screamed in a faint, furious voice as I walked away at speed.

EIGHTEEN

August 17 was a strangely cool day, dawning clear and windy, as if the heat had finally grown a little tired of itself and decided to sit things out and fan itself with a hand. Visibility was excellent from the attic window, and my morning telescopic security sweep netted me two dog-walkers and a man mowing his lawn into violent green stripes. I screwed on the Barlow lens, doubling my magnification, and through the kitchen window of a distant house saw what appeared to be a laughing, very young girl forcing her brother's face into a bowl.

After carefully block-printing this into my logbook I went downstairs, eager to check on Vietnam. As the summer went on it had become a habit, a kind of need. I had grown used to the announcers with their breezeway haircuts and careful fake voices speaking about kill ratios and body counts, but I could never get enough of the war itself. At least twice a day I now crouched in front of the television, watching thrilling dragonfly helicopters darting in for the kill while fighter jets roared overhead and soldiers dashed to and fro in the forest, dropping quick to one knee to shoot bright, star-shaped bursts out the ends of their guns.

And yet, as great as the war was to watch, on that day,

August 17, I became officially disgusted with the war. I saw a wounded soldier carried into a clearing in a blanket by men on the run, and as I watched, the men stopped suddenly and a leg flew out of the blanket and stood up on the ground by itself for a second, and though the camera cut quickly away, I felt a throb in my guts like I was going to vomit, and I had to stand up myself and walk around the room until I felt better. When I had calmed down, I came to a spontaneous decision: Call Sabina. It had only been a few days since I'd dismantled her doll, but I suddenly wanted to look into her clean, living face, to make her laugh and to try talking to her out of the new windy science that had recently begun flowing through my body. I had this vague idea I wanted to try out on the deeply groomed, well-spoken girl who lived around the corner.

Actually it wasn't vague at all.

I dialed her number, and when she heard my voice, she shouted, "*Che piacére!* And then said, "Denny! I'm so happy you called. How are you?"

"Fine," I said, "but I was wondering today, if maybe sometime, like later or something, you might want to . . . to . . ."

"What, Denny? Meet?"

"Yes."

"Sour or sweet?"

"Excuse me?"

"It's something my sister always says. Do you want to get something sour to eat, like a hamburger with pickles, or something sweet, like ice cream."

"Sweet, I guess."

"Me, too. Taylor's?"

"Sure."

Taylor's Dairy was a luncheonette near our homes that sat on a stream and pretended to be someone's incredibly clean, incredibly white house even though it was actually a restaurant filled with ice cream and waitresses and the drool-producing smell of grilling meat. Also there were barns attached, and big lawns behind where the cows grazed. I loved cows. They had long lashes and seven stomachs, and to make things even better, I had once watched a movie of them being killed. The bolt of electricity that stunned them sent them instantly to the floor, legs buckling. Then they were hosed down, sawed up, whisked into shrink-wrapped packages, placed under the broilers, and cooked by a flame whose color, I'd recently learned, was *gentian*.

I went to take a shower, and then got dressed in shorts and a T-shirt and set out. Arriving at Taylor's first, I slid into a booth, and a few seconds later Sabina entered the restaurant, wearing a powder-blue dress and white patent leather shoes with little straps and gold buckles. She waved hello, and as she came toward me she said, "In Italy, we greet one another by saying, 'How does it go?' And so, how does it?"

"Fine," I lied, as she slipped into the booth across from me. I dropped my eyes and stared at the ragged crescents of my nails, bitten that morning so that they'd bled afresh.

"You look better," she said. "Are you more relaxed than the last time I saw you?"

"I don't feel relaxed."

"Maybe I can help," she said, and smiled. The waitress came over and began to place the menus in front of us, but Sabina, in her high, crisp voice said, "Two root beer floats, if you please." The waitress looked at her a second, squinting, and then turned away. When she was gone, Sabina leaned toward me.

"I hope you don't mind," she said.

"No, I like root beer."

"Good, and I have a surprise for you."

ELI GOTTLIEB

"Really?"

"Really." She bent over, and from below the table extracted a paper bag. "Here," she said with a little grunt, hefting the bag to the center of the table.

"What is it?"

"Ah, now I'll show you." From the bag she withdrew a large, worn leather photo album that was decorated with elaborate raised fleur de lis.

"This is the official record of our family," she said, and opened the book and placed her hand on a page. I looked at the hand, and at each of its slender fingers, ending in a perfect little fluted chip of nail.

"We're a very old family, that goes all the way back to dukes and duchesses. Did you know that? Here." She spun the book around with her finger on a faded photo of an old, bent woman dressed entirely in black. "This is Nonna Marella, my grandma, but we called her Nonna Mortadella, like the big salami, because she had a dangerous long love affair with the town butcher." Sabina gave a little laugh.

I tried my new fake smile, which consisted of raising my upper lip till I felt the air on my teeth.

"Jeez," I said faintly.

"And this," she said, turning one of the big stiff pages and pointing, "is Uncle Giuseppe. Isn't he handsome?" I saw a middle-aged man with slicked-back hair and a bigger, boxier suit than Max's.

"Yeah," I said, "but Sabina?"

"Yes?" She looked up at me, bright-eyed. Her face seemed to be drawn upward, as if pinned behind the neck.

"This 'affair' you talked about with your grandmother?" I tried to sound casual. "Uh, why do you think it happened?"

"Why? Well, these are family secrets, you know. But we girls thought it was because her husband treated her so badly.

In Italy, in the old times, it was very hard to get a divorce. You had to go to a priest and make enormous problems for everybody. The whole town would know. So, they would do this other thing."

"What?"

"Have what we call *avventure*. Love stories."

"And these love stories, what did you think about them yourself?" I asked boldly.

"Well"—she flared her nostrils—"they are dangerous, and they are stupid, too. Marriage is a sacred vow, you know. And if you think you're being watched from up in the sky when you walk around your house, imagine how closely they're watching you when you take your wedding vows."

"Who?"

She flung a finger straight up in the air. "Them. The souls. The judges."

"Ah."

I went very slowly.

"Sabina," I said, "I kinda think you should know something."

"Really, what's that?"

"It has to do with my mother."

"Yes, tell me." She crimped her mouth around the straw, began to suck ice water from her glass. I watched it rise, flowing upward in the straw.

"My mother, you see, she's doing something."

Sabina laughed. "I'm sure she is, Denny."

"No, I mean something not right, sort of."

The clear liquid retreated back down the straw.

"What do you mean?"

"I mean," taking a deep breath, "that she's having an affair."

Sabina rocked back as if struck, her eyes widening in her head. "Mrs. Graubart?" she breathed.

I slowly nodded up and down.

"Harta Graubart, my mom."

She gripped the table edge with both hands.

"Now wait, Denny. Just hold on. Are you saying that your mother is having a love affair—I mean apart from the love affair with your father?"

"Yes." I felt great suddenly. "I'm sure of it."

Never taking her eyes away from mine, Sabina groped a moment in the air, finding her straw, and then sucked the last of the water from her glass.

"No," she said softly. "It can't be." The wind was blowing harder now, fizzing steadily in my nerves. It wanted Sabina to look at me. It wanted her to respect me. It wanted her to understand that the glossy, wisecracking athletes of my school to whom I was a "stain," in the language of the school corridors, were completely mistaken in their opinions. In a strange, deep, confident adult voice it remembered from television, the wind said, "You see, Sabina, I have a little hobby. I do things around the house."

"What do you mean?" she asked.

"I mean that I study the things that go on around the house, and make notes about them."

"Why? I still don't understand."

"Sabina"—I drew a deep, exhausted breath—"I'm a spy."

"A spy?" The open look on her face suddenly snapped shut. She rocked back in her chair and, to my disappointment, she laughed out loud—a high silvery sound, as of pocket change falling through the air. As I watched, she quickly extended her hands so far forward they nearly touched my face.

"I'm sorry. It's just so funny to hear you say it like that, 'a spy.' Denny, you're really nutty, you know?" She erupted in a cascade of giggles again. "Upon whom do you—do you spy?"

"Them—my parents and brother. And"—I hurried on before she could laugh again—"I discovered this love story while spying one afternoon."

"Oh, Denny." She shook her head. "Oh, poor Denny."

"What do you mean?" I asked.

"I mean that I'm sure you're wrong, *tesoro mio*. Your mother is a lovely, polite person. You live in a nice house, and your brother is troubled, yes, but he goes to a very good school for it. I know he does, because your mother told my mother all about it. So, you see, it's all quite simple: You're wrong."

"Sabina, I'm telling you. I *know* she is having one."

"An affair."

"*Yes*, an affair."

Sabina sighed, looked down, and then flung her head back up again. A split-second later, her hair flung itself after her.

"The last time I saw you, you hinted that things at your house were not going well," she said crisply. "Now you come out with these crazy ideas. Your mother and other men. Do you even know what an *affair* is? Do you know what happens in an *affair*?"

"Of course I do. The man and the woman get together, and then they . . . get together." A familiar thick feeling engulfed my brain.

This time Sabina's laugh was not so silvery. It was hard and grinding and it went on and on as I slowly sank beneath the table. At last, recovering in little flurries of breath, she placed her hand at her throat.

"Denny," she said, gasping a little. "They always told

me that girls grew up before boys, and I was never sure until now. Maybe you need something to do with your time. Have you thought about a paper route?"

I sank a little lower.

"Okay, I'm sorry," said Sabina, her expression alternating with fascinating speed between frowns and spurts of helpless laughter. "That wasn't nice. But Denny, I assure you that these ideas of yours are not correct. Have you told anyone else about them?"

"No, you're the very first."

"I think you should keep it that way. There is no affair and you're a very silly boy," said giggling Sabina, putting her perfectly manicured hand in front of her mouth. I sat back in my chair, smiling weakly as the root beer floats arrived. Sabina ate her ice cream quickly and efficiently, spearing it on her long-handled spoon and popping it into her mouth. I watched for a while, and then, coming to a decision that I had to speak, I cleared my throat, leaned forward with a confident feeling on my face, and brought my hands up in the air on either side of my head like a person climbing a ladder. "Sabina," I said, and then realized a very specific thing: I had no idea what I wanted to say, and the wind, though I felt around for it in my head for several long seconds, was nowhere to be found.

NINETEEN

The very next morning, the summons arrived. I was ready for the summons. I had been waiting for the summons for weeks, after all, even in a sense for months. I was sitting that morning at the kitchen table dressed in my best robin's-egg-blue pajamas, pressing the tips of my fingers together like Max and nesting my chin in them. The family was spread around me at breakfast, eating quietly. Everything was almost perfect. Everything was going according to plan. And yet something was in the air that morning. I shut my eyes a moment and felt the something. It felt, I had to admit, like something pretty big.

"Hoss," said Harta, drenching a steaming stack of pancakes with maple syrup, forking a thick wedge of them, and beginning to chew with muscular squeaks of the jaw, "I'd like you to ride shotgun this afternoon."

"Where to?" I asked.

"A doctor-man." She licked a tear of syrup off her lip. "To heal up one of our hurt cowpokes."

"Stop it, Mom. You're not funny. Which one?"

"Dr. Minkoff," she said quickly, "for James's annual physical." I looked up to see if she showed any emotion on her face, like phony smiles or frowns. There were none that I could see, but Max, sitting at the table behind the screen of *The Times*, gave a long, drawn-out clearing of the throat—the most he'd said at the table in several days.

Minkoff!

As soon as Max left the table, I excused myself and went to call Derwent. I hadn't spoken to him since the incident at his house with the jerk-off tunnel and was a little nervous, but I needed to talk. Derwent answered the phone and immediately said in a snide, nasty voice, "We-el, if it isn't little Miss Muffet from up the hill. How's everything back in puberty?"

"Hey, Derwent, don't have a cow. I just kinda needed to leave that day. And besides, it's D-Day this afternoon."

"How's that, Pudd'nhead?"

"We're going to see Minkoff."

"You're what?" he shouted.

"We're seeing the guy today for Fad's physical."

"Christ is risen from the grave," he intoned in a loud voice, "to fish for our souls." Then, as if nothing had happened, he cried. "That's great, Dad! The visit at last! Okay, now hang on." There was a riffle of papers. "Right, Minkoff. Now listen carefully to me here, because I can't afford a screwup. Here's what I want: eye contact, but not too much; friendliness, but only up to a point. Blend in, get it? And if things get out of control, always remember: You're the younger brother of an authentic genetic fuckup and entitled to be a little weird."

I didn't say anything.

"Most important of all, bring a small notepad with you, and excuse yourself to take a piss and then get everything— I mean everything you can. Names and numbers, addresses and descriptions. I want the place cased and inventoried."

"Fine," I said, "but like for what, exactly?"

"Crabmeat," Derwent said in a favorite mangling of my surname, "it pains me to have to say this to you, but you're a moron, and as such deserve no further explanation. Just go out and do what I say," he said wearily, "and leave the thinking to me."

For the next several hours I paced irritably, unable to do work of any sort. The shadows lengthened in my room as if in pursuit of something. The sun rode around the house. Finally, at 4 P.M., Harta's singsong voice summoned me to the front door and we left in the Corvair. Ten minutes of driving on familiar sleepy streets brought us to the divide of Bloomfield Avenue, where the calm spaces of our neighborhood gave way to taller buildings, pedestrians, the dots and zigzags of streaking neon, and cars rushing by as if fleeing for their lives. Harta drove with yanks of the steering wheel down several side streets, and we soon entered the parking lot of a small office building, where the sign MEDICAL ARTS sat high on a pole, dividing the warm summer wind. As we got out and stood near the car a moment, I stared at Minkoff's name on the sign, feeling a band of tension tightening around my chest. Meanwhile, Harta was brushing Fad's hair with a hand and straightening his stiff new white shirt while whispering something to him I couldn't hear. When they were ready, we walked together up a flight of steps, entered a cool, dim building, and spoke to an elderly woman sitting behind a curved desk. A moment later, all three of us together were ushered down a hallway into an examining room. It was here that The Suspect, his back to us, turned around with a smile as we entered the door.

Dr. Minkoff was a short, fat, sweating man of about fifty, with Coke-bottle glasses, rabbit-pink skin, and a sneezy expression on his face of just having scratched a major itch and waiting for it to itch again. He didn't look like a doctor at all.

He looked like another kind of person entirely—a smaller, more frazzled, more familiar person. Although I had burned with thoughts of killing him for days, the only thing I could do when I finally met Minkoff face-to-face was laugh.

I covered my snicker with a cough, but not fast enough.

"I'm glad to see your son finds me so amusing," said the doctor, with a fixed smile on his face. His gaze lit on Fad, who was just then energetically biting his hand, and his smile widened.

"And this," he said, bending forward and cracking his knuckles briskly, "must be the man of the hour."

Harta pushed out the front of her body to urge Fad ahead, while I walked behind them into the examining room, turning my face to either side, slowly and methodically.

"This is the one, Doctor!" she cried.

My vision drew to the center. Fad was holding soiled hands to his face, had made a square hole of his fingers, and was peering through it like a movie director framing a shot.

"I can see you," he said to the doctor in a tone of deep disappointment.

The doctor's smile shriveled.

"We're here today to do a physical," he said, clearing his throat. "If you were a car we'd call it a tune-up. Do you like cars?"

No one said a word. Usually I wasn't allowed in examining rooms, but I had gotten this far and I wasn't about to leave yet. I shrank back against the wall, watching closely.

"Right," said the doctor, walking to a cabinet and removing a small glittering tube. "This," he said, "is called an eye scope. I bet you know what it's for, don't you?"

The doctor bent forward at the waist, lowering himself until his face was in front of Fad's, and then slowly raising the eye scope into position.

"Mom," said Fad in a chill, flat voice.

"Yes?"

"How will the man be if I spit at him?"

"I'm sure he'll be very upset," she said, and forced a laugh.

The doctor squinted into his instrument, plying a needle of light around Fad's eye.

"Well," he said with a chuckle, "I've been peed on enough times, and worse, too. But spit on? Not yet anyway."

Dr. Minkoff stood up, sighing, and steepled his hands over his breastbone.

"Your mother," said the doctor delicately, "explained to me that you're the type of young man who likes to know what's being done to you, so I'm going to tell you that the blood test gives a tiny pain, like a fly bite, but it's very important, okay?"

"No!" cried Fad.

Harta seemed to awaken then, tilting her head gravely to the side while her long, lariatlike arms flowed around Fad's body and drew him close. Tenderly she whispered into the horn of his ear in a burring soft voice that he was a best boy, one of the very best boys in all the world.

"There's never been a boy in the history of the universe as handsome and as well behaved in doctors' offices as you," she said softly. "And never a mom as lucky as I am to have you."

Fad was just turning to her with a smile on his face when the door opened and the nurse came in—a large, square, red-faced person atop whose head, like a wave breaking, was set a fluted white cap. She aimed the cap at Fad.

"This the little blood-giver?" she asked.

"Say hi," said Harta.

"Hi." His voice fell down as he said it.

The nurse opened her bag, exposing odd loops of rubber

tubing, glass pipettes, and gauges. She took out a small white cotton swab, wiped Fad's index finger, and then stared at him a moment.

"Aren't you a handsome young man," she said loudly, smiling as she stabbed a bright piece of metal fast into the pad of his finger. From a great, bored distance I observed the widening hoop of bewilderment passing over Fad's face as the pain rang in from the remote station of his finger, grew up fast into a genuine sting.

He screamed, a good, solid, meat-eating burst of sound. But the nurse, though he began to struggle, hung on and sucked the blood in a thin red line up the pipette. She bound his finger with a piece of gauze and a Band-Aid, while Harta tenderly stroked his brow and winked in my direction.

Excusing myself, I went to the bathroom and turned on the water in the sink. Then, withdrawing my pad, I wrote down everything I could think of about the doctor. I described the strange piney smell of his offices, and the way the doors whizzed shut with a sound of asthma. I mentioned his nurse, whom I named "Miss Mosler" for the safe she resembled, and the elderly receptionist behind her curved console. I made a rough sketch of the branching floor plan of the offices, described the lighting (fluorescent), the carpet (turd-hued indoor-outdoor), and the two emergency exits in the middle of the hall.

When I got back to the examining room Fad was buttoning up his shirt and Harta was smiling at Dr. Minkoff like he'd just swum to shore from a sinking ship with a sick baby in his mouth. The doctor was saying that Fad was in "super shape," and I pretended not to notice the way her eyes glistened or her whole body bent forward as she listened. I said good-bye to Minkoff as if it were the most normal thing in the world, and the three of us walked out and back to the car. On the way home, I lay in the backseat while Fad sat in front, rocking, crooning, and whickering.

"That wasn't so awful, was it, baby?" asked Harta as she drove.

Fad, blowing her guilt like a trumpet, cried instantly, "Can I have a milk shake?"

"Not now, honey, you have dinner coming up."

"The doctor is a bad man!" he shouted.

"The doctor is not a bad man," she said with an odd, forced music in her voice, like she was carrying the words up a slight grade. "He's a very good man. And you want to know something else?"

"No!"

"He cares very much about you," she said. "He took me aside afterward and went on and on about what an exceptionally intelligent young man you are."

"I," said Fad evenly, "am an exceptionally intelligent young man."

"What else did he say, Mom?" I asked from the backseat.

"What about?" Harta kept her eyes on the road.

"Oh, anything," I said.

Silence. And then: "We talked about this and that. He was very interested to meet you."

"Why?"

"Well, he'd heard so much about you."

"I thought this was the first time you were seeing him."

Harta kept her eyes steadily on the road.

"No, we've been in contact before."

"On the phone?"

She laughed. "Do you know the term *third degree*, honey?"

"No."

"It's when people ask lots of questions of another person in a hostile way. Usually lawyers do it. Not children like you, Denty Moore."

On reflex, I felt in my pocket where the pad bearing all my notes was hidden. It was there. I relaxed.

"Sure," I said, "I knew that."

TWENTY

In the wake of our Minkoff visit, Max continued moving as if on a planet with a slower, sadder, heavier gravity than our own. But Harta was bristling and glowing, leaving often for appointments and trailing extravagant new perfumes in her wake. And she was cleaning. I had never noticed her cleaning before. And yet suddenly the scattered objects on the floor of my room were whisked out of sight; the disheveled piles of towels in the closet were piled neat. With her latest hairstyle, a "Carol Channing," Harta seemed everywhere at once, rag in hand. In the space of a single afternoon I watched her wiping half-moons of dust from the corner, flicking a cloth between the legs of our "authentic" Michelangelo's *David*, and polishing the wooden kitchen table with Lemon Pledge and giant, squeaking sweeps of the arm.

"It's for this Comprehensive Exam thing," Harta said over the phone to Maude that same evening, cooking dinner. I sat listening on the phone in the basement, my feet propped on a chair and a notebook in my hand, idly eating a Drake's Devil Dog.

"I need the house as neat as a pin," said Harta. "You want to know why? Because these doctors, these 'experts,'

150 these Einsteins in Trenton ask him questions about his personal hygiene, his room, and even his laundry is why! Can you imagine the nerve?"

The televisions in both houses, at the very same time, said the words, "Hanoi Hilton."

"You sound so nervous, Hartie," Maude said.

"How could I not be, honey? I mean, really." Harta threw something on a pan that began to hiss and spit.

"What do they test him on?"

"Just about everything—neuro, psycho, bio, the works. It's the big state-level people, a whole gang of these *machers* assembled for the day. And what they say goes."

"And what can 'they' say?"

"Maude, darling, don't you understand? They can say no."

"No?"

"To everything." Her voice wavered. After a moment, she said sadly, "Without their say-so, the state funding dries up. And if we get no money for day schools, there's really not much of an alternative to sending him away to a place like Ramphill Village. I'm afraid it's all in the hands of these people."

"But—but what are you going to do?"

"Do? What *can* I do? I'm doing everything, doll. And as fast as I can."

To the neatening of our house, and the regular two- or three-times-daily session of home training with Fad, Harta now added something called positive reinforcement therapy. This, she'd explained to Maude, was "the last word" in behavioral home therapy, and would be "an absolute cincheroo" to put Fad in a good mood for his big day with the examiners. Apparently, the idea was to keep my brother so happy all the time that he wouldn't have the time to recall the fundamental fact: He was nuts. And so, after days of doing very little to-gether as a threesome, we suddenly began doing tons.

We went to the Palisades Amusement Park and rode the log flume through walls of crashing water, were spun in the Tilt-A-Whirl and banged silly in the bumper cars. At Teterboro Airport, we took a sight-seeing trip in a small plane, jerking straight into the air and then drifting sideways over a landscape that looked like heaped broccoli. The point was to keep Fad's mind open, easy, and full of new sights and sounds. But Harta was at work not only on his mind. With me being dragged reluctantly behind, we drove to Duboff's Mens and Boys, where she purchased him a new suit, boxy just like Max's. In another store, she bought him shiny new shoes and a tie like a spurt of blood. His hair, on a daily basis, was slicked back in a glistening hood. His teeth sparkled when he talked. Harta had done research on the Comprehensive Exam, and found out that Fad would be required to present responses to imaginary situations of danger and difficulty, so she added a series of lessons specifically for that.

I had for the most part lost interest in watching my mother and brother at their home lessons. Too many other things were happening for me to remain focused on the show a room away. Nonetheless, every few days I'd peer through the hole in my closet and take a peek. Dependably, I'd see Fad sagging against a doorframe, his new pants bagged on his shoes. His hair shone. His crisp clean shirt was as white as a sail. He looked like someone about to go out on a job interview, run for class president, sing in the church choir—until, that is, you drew nearer, looked in his eyes, and realized the truth: He wasn't there at all.

"Darling," said Harta softly. "Sweetpea," she said with a new tenderness in her voice. It seemed that as the summer went on she was filled with love for Fad that was so great it nearly burst her heart. "Bananacake, it's time for some role-playing."

Standing rigid in the middle of the room, he stared indifferently into space.

"I want to talk about crisis," she said softly.

"Inside horses," Fad whispered to himself, "is blood."

"Now," she said. "Let's say you are lying in the backyard, under the willow tree, and after a while you get thirsty."

"Thirsty, Mommy?" Fad returned abruptly to attention.

"Yes, and you decide to come in for some water."

"No, Fanta Orange!"

"Water, darling, and when you come inside you see Mommy and I'm lying on the floor and my face is all purple like someone splashed me with grape Kool-Aid. I'm making sounds. What do you do?"

Fad stared calmly at her. After a moment, with no change of expression, he sighed.

"Argh, baby! Urgh!" cried Harta. "I'm choking, honey. I can't breathe! Who do you call—quick, it's a crisis—what do you do?"

Her body was large, shaped like the soft inlapped curves of certain natural formations I'd seen in TV documentaries of the Utah Desert. When Fad said nothing, Harta, perturbed, put her hands on her hips. Her hips. In each of them, according to the marriage manual, was a flower of sex with a curved spout to it through which the seed of the baby passed: *ovary*.

"Honey," she said, "if you don't do something very specific, like run to the phone and then tell the policeman who you are, and where you live, and what color your Mommy's face is, then your Mommy will die."

Die? I thought to myself. *Die?*

"You don't want Mommy to die, do you?"

"Noooo," said Fad suddenly, sucking in the breath like a long spaghetti strand.

"Well, if you don't want Mommy to die, then you must absolutely get very clear about crisis. You dial the police, first, as I just told you. What's the number?"

"I don't know."

"O for Operator, okay?"

"Mommy?"

"Yes."

"There's just a teeny bit of me left."

"Stop talking nonsense, please." With a sigh, Harta got up and left the frame of my vision. When she returned, a moment later, she was wearing a derby that rose straight up in the air, as if surprised. Beneath this derby, she had crimped her face into an expression of great seriousness. She had slitted her eyes, and made herself jowly by pulling her head back on her neck.

"Harrumph!" she cried in a deep voice. "I'm the very busy Dr. Feinstein, and you must be James Graubart. Good morning to you and welcome."

Fad, who had been rocking in place, suddenly stopped and gave his fake smile. Leaning forward as if he were about to topple over, he clenched both hands, flung himself upright, and shouted, "Good morning, Doctor!"

"Pleased to meet you," said Harta, "Won't you sit down?"

With no ado, he dropped thudding onto the carpet.

"This is a very important day for you, because your mother," said Harta with a strained smile, "has asked you to come to me so that we could discuss how you're doing. I'm a doctor, a very powerful man, and I have very little time. Now, ahem!" She cleared her throat importantly. "I'd like to tell you that you seem very calm and happy. Is that correct?"

"Mommy, can I see your peeper?"

Harta shut her eyes for a long time. With her eyes still closed, she said, "Young man, I don't think you understand the seriousness of the situation, do you? I have only a limited amount of time to spend with you, and it's important that you impress me with how well behaved and adjusted you are. I understand you're very happy being a boy who lives at home with his mommy and his daddy and his brother. Is that true?"

"I don't know," said Fad.

"No, I'm telling you, you *do* live happily at home with them. Mr. Graubart, could you repeat that after me, please?"

"Daddy's Mr. Graubart," Fad crowed delightedly. "I'm James!"

"Okay, James, could you repeat what I just said?"

Instead, sitting on the floor, he began rocking back and forth, accelerating as I watched. It was as if he were struggling to get somewhere, to throw himself like an object right out of the present tense. For a second he stopped and sat breathless, as if unsure what to do next, and then fell heavily over on one side.

"I hope you're pleased with your little show, James," came Harta's normal voice. "Now, young man," she said in the doctor's baritone, "let us return to our discussion. I was saying that I was impressed by what a happy, calm young man you are. Clearly, you're having a good time staying at home. Is that right?"

Lying on his side, he opened his hand, placed the palm of it in front of his face, and began whispering into it confidingly.

"Son, I have to warn you that I'm a very busy man, and I cannot tolerate this kind of behavior much longer. If you behave correctly with me, however, it's possible that my nurse

Mrs. McGillicuddy will give you a very big glass of chocolate milk."

Fad sat bolt upright, eyes flashing.

"Bosco, Mommy!"

"Okay," said Harta, pleased with his return to attention. "Now let's continue our questioning. Tell me, young man, do you feel comfortable at home? Do you have friends that you can talk to? Are you ever"—her voice had taken on the drone that indicated she was reading, though I couldn't quite see what—"frightened at night so badly you feel you *have* to talk to somebody? Do you sleep well? Do you eat well? Are you happy at home, James Graubart?"

"I want it to be a wooden world that stays in one place so I can touch it whenever I want to!"

"I'm waiting, James."

"Denny Graubart is my brother and Max Graubart is my father. Max Graubart talks in a low voice in my head sometimes that makes me want to cry."

"I'm sure he doesn't do that on purpose, does he? I'm sure he's a very kind and loving man. Son? Are you listening? I say I'm sure your father loves you very much. Isn't that true?"

"Pants are for wearing, paper for tearing," whispered Fad to himself, "the other way around is upside down. Mommy," he said in a loud voice, "when I'm dead can I have some cotton candy?"

"Your brother and your father love you very much, James. Don't you know that?"

"I want to touch girls somewhere in their bodies."

Harta's voice was beginning to rise. She was speaking under a terrible pressure of some sort, a force that threatened her control, word by word, phrase by phrase.

"Don't you understand, darling? You simply *must* pay attention. We're here to prepare you for the real doctor, next week. It's *so* important, James. You have got to learn to sit there and be perfectly behaved. Concentrate hard. No flying away. No drifting with your head."

"Clouds in my head!"

"No!" she said sharply. "Not today, Jimmy. And no wheeing, either. Do you understand?"

Fad, back up in a sitting position, said nothing, and then, after a moment of silence, staring at Harta, seemed to make a great effort of concentration.

"Cashew," he said.

Harta's eyes flew terribly wide open in her head. *"DO YOU UNDERSTAND?"* she screamed, louder than I'd heard her ever scream, and then slowly lowered her face into her hands. Fad, as if physically recoiling from the sound, flung himself backward out of my frame of vision. Though I couldn't see him, I could hear clearly. He was doing what he so often did when she screamed (which was why she so rarely did it): attack himself. The soft ripping sounds of flesh being fanged, the grunts and pants as he tore holes in his hand—these noises were as familiar to me as the Mozart operas of tiny clear voices flowing with what seemed permanent hysteria from the cloth-of-gold speakers in the living room. I stirred involuntarily, there at the hole, as Harta, raising her head, transformed her weepy face to anger as hard and pointed as a pylon.

"Goddamn you, *stop it!*" she screamed, lunging toward him, sprinting across the room; and finally, satisfyingly, using her weight. She lowered her shoulder and hit him in the chest with a blow that lifted him right off the ground and flung him into the wall with a thud I felt in my own body. Stunned for a second, he looked at her, amazed, and then screamed a single loud scream, a yell of rebellion and contempt, and sank his teeth as deeply as he could into his hand.

Swinging her right arm like a prizefighter, she grabbed him by the hair and jerked him backward hard, causing flecks of blood to fly up the wall. Blood seemed to be everywhere, crudely lipsticking his mouth, spattered on the wall, and flung in bright little galaxies of droplets on the cream-colored carpeting. But Harta, after standing open-mouthed a second, blinking, was suddenly reaching for him, pulling his head toward her breast, and shouting, "Don't you know I love you? I love you, don't you know that?" She grabbed his bloody head by the ears and from an inch away cried, "You're the most precious thing in the world to me, darling, don't you know that?"

There was a silence, a moment's pause as his head flew back on his neck and he took a deep, racking breath, getting ready to scream. I looked down, giggling uncontrollably.

An erection was straining the cloth of my trousers.

SEPTEMBER

TWENTY-ONE

In the night the dark was very dark, and the quiet very quiet. Standing at the edge of the parking lot, we could hear the faint buzz of the fluorescent lights. The only other sound was an almost inaudible hissing in the atmosphere, as if the pressurized air of the planet were being sprayed out of a can. I stuck my tongue out into the air. It was the same air that was just then drifting over the outlines of nearby houses, fingering the zillionfold leaves of trees. In beds, in rooms all over town, this air was crawling lewdly up and down the soft, forked forms of women.

We waited until the nearby street was empty of passing cars, then ran up the stairs, jiggled the pick in the lock for five minutes, and stood back a moment. The door to Minkoff's offices swung open with a wheeze.

"Sex and filth dead ahead," whispered Derwent, turning to me with a gigantic smile. Giggling, I followed him through the entrance and into the waiting room, the bright wand of light from his flashlight turning up the familiar details of curved console, rigidly arranged chairs of the waiting room, ladders of magazine racks bulging with dog-eared issues. It was all exactly as I remembered it. And though a slithering midnight escape from my bedroom window and a half-hour bicycle ride had brought me here, it seemed I had been waiting many months or even years to crouch in this particular dimness, mouth open, blood thudding at my temples with slow heavy beats.

I looked up. Derwent had gone off into a side room, from which I soon heard the squeak of a large file cabinet being opened, and then the feathery rush of files falling to the floor. I walked into the nearest office, which was almost entirely dark, took a deep breath, and withdrew the BB pistol from a coat pocket. Without pointing it anywhere in particular, I pulled the trigger. Instantly there was a small splatting noise followed by a running tinkle. I pulled again, producing a crisp, conclusive sound somewhat closer to a *clank!* Wheeling around, I winged a small canister of tongue depressors. I shattered the glass front of a locked medicine cabinet, and then, ducking into the next room down the hall, sent BB's spraying off the beaked metal breast of the X-ray machine.

This is for you, said a voice in my head, as I squeezed off shots into Minkoff's picture windows, and this and this, said the voice as I exploded his collection of family photographs, and demolished his large collection of brownish vases and the desktop statues of women with the immense breasts and hips I imagined were produced by a lifetime of eating only dessert. My heart seemed to unlatch itself, to drift free of my chest in happiness as I perforated the magazines in their racks, and with a single well-aimed BB let the wind permanently out of the sails of his painted clipper ship.

"The boinking most likely takes place on this couch," called Derwent from somewhere in the dimness. I stopped, holding my red-hot pistol, and walked uneasily away from the direction of his voice. I was here to destroy, not draw near anything to do with *that:* the act, the thing they actually did together, the moment, biweekly if Derwent were correct, when the naked, bushy-haired Doctor Minkoff climbed on Harta and in some unspeakable way sawed her in two. I recovered my nerve, loaded another compressed gas canister into the gun, and continued blasting away. Ten minutes later, Derwent came up to me, leaned forward, and loudly and clearly whispered the word "snuff!" Slapping hands, laughing wildly, we left.

The first thing I noticed the next morning was the light. It was not the regular calming flood of yolk-colored early sunshine, but something pointed and specific, as if the cheery beams had been individually tipped with thrusting fingers. I sat up in bed and looked around. Everything was overclear, abnormally detailed, strangely lit from within. When I dressed and went downstairs I was amazed at the quiet, the calm, the orderly normal way in which Max, at breakfast, said absolutely nothing; Harta, muted, went about preparing eggs; Fad, groaning, rocked to and fro. I had never noticed just how beautiful it was to walk slowly upstairs after everyone else had left on their errands, to swing the long telescope around on its tripod and begin my normal day's surveillance. My hands were shaking slightly and I could hear my breath rasping in my throat from fear, but I told myself that this was exactly what I was supposed to feel. I was a criminal and everything was wonderful.

When Harta came in later that day and asked if I could "stay on top of things" for a while because Max was going to be working in the basement and she was going to the hairdresser, I said, "Sure, I'll hold the fort," in the most natural voice in the world. She left, driving, though she could have walked. As the sound of her car trailed away down the hill, I fell back in bed, book in hand. But I was unable to concentrate on reading. Instead, I rehearsed in my mind's eye the scenario of Minkoff's arrival that morning at work. I imagined him, horn-haired, potbellied, twisting the wheel of his gigantic Lincoln Continental as he rolled into his parking lot, sat a moment resting on the tufted cushions, and felt a faint tickling in the corner of his visual field. He turned, looked up at his row of smashed office windows, and felt all the blood in his body stop on the spot.

The phone rang for what, according to my calculations, was the sixty-third time that week. I calmly put my book down and went to get it.

"Hello," said a familiar, slightly nasal voice. "Is Mrs. Graubart there?"

"No, I'm sorry, she's at the hairdresser now, but she'll be back in about an hour."

"An hour, I see. Okay, I'll call her back then. Thank you."

"Who's calling?" I asked.

There was a pause, a beat too long.

"Dr. Minkoff," he said slowly. "And you must be—"

"Denny."

"Young Denny, of course of course. How are you?"

"Fine."

"Always good to hear. And your brother?"

"He's fine, too."

"Well then," said the doctor with sudden briskness, "I'll be seeing you soon. Keep those tonsils of yours in tip-top shape, and please tell your mother I called."

"Sure," I said, and hung up with a whamming heart. Instantly I leaped from the sofa and began to pace. I used the hallway for this, because no one was there and I enjoyed the nubbly feeling of the carpeting underfoot. He knew something, the doctor did, but what exactly? I paced back and forth on the carpet, wondering over the possibilities, and when I finally heard Harta's car crawling up the hill with a sustained sucking sound, I readied myself in a pose of Maximum Relax on the overstuffed easy chair, faced front and center, and awaited her arrival with fraudulent calm. Up the driveway she came, transmission ratcheting into Park, engine humming a moment as she opened the garage door with her powerful body, and then the car rolled slowly into the garage.

I smiled, lacing my trembling hands through each other. A moment later Harta entered through a side door, stopped in front of me, and turned, holding her lip between her teeth, while crying, "Dah-dah! How do you like it?"

The unmistakable smell whirled around the room as she spun—conditioner and hot lights burning, protein rinse and Dippity-Do.

"It looks nice," I said wanly.

"He gave me a French flip, honey."

"Oh." I wasn't sure what this was, but I nodded anyway.

"And I brought back some delicious steaks for us tonight."

"Wow, great!" I faked. Concentrating hard as she walked away from me, I said, "Oh, and Mom?"

She turned.

"Dr. Minkoff called."

"Yeah?"

"Yah, he sounded a little weird, too."

"Weird, baby? How?"

"I don't know, maybe like he was upset sort of."

I was a smooth, a natural liar.

"Like he was upset? Are you sure?"

"I don't know, Mom. He seemed weird."

Beneath the gleaming geometric solid of her hair, she

seemed to grow thoughtful. Then her expression brightened. "How's for some lunch?"

"Sure."

"Where's your brother?"

I pointed my finger upstairs and let my eyes slide down the length of my upstanding arm and back to my book.

As soon as she was out of sight, however, I arose silently and stole on shaking legs downstairs to my basement listening post, where I picked up the phone patch, certain she'd call him right back. I was correct in my hunch, for as I picked up I heard a nursey voice saying, "One minute, I'll have to find him," and was then treated to the nervous inhalations of Harta's for the next thirty seconds. I grabbed my pen, opened up the appropriate page.

Presently Minkoff, in his oily voice, inquired: "Yes, how can I help you?"

"This is Mrs. Graubart."

"Ah, Mrs. Graubart." The voice tautened unmistakably.

"I was told by my son that you'd called, and I wondered if it was anything urgent."

"Yes, it was after a fashion. Do you think you could hold the line a second?"

"Certainly." She began to hum as she waited, and was still humming when the line clicked suddenly into a newer, more treble atmosphere.

"Listen," came the voice.

"I'm all yours," she said girlishly.

"No, really. I have something serious here. I—I do you—I mean this is slightly unbelievable, actually."

"What, darling? Tell me."

"I'll make it short and to the point. I was coming into work this morning, everything's fine, right, and then I pull into the parking lot, and I look up and see this—these windows of mine, that are totally shattered.

"What? You mean somebody threw rocks?"

Minkoff laughed strangely. "I wish. No, this was a little more specific."

"How so?" asked Harta.

The doctor drew a deep breath. "They ransacked my office."

"They what?"

"Files destroyed, cabinets broken, paintings slashed. Harta, the place looks like a bomb fell. I don't know where to begin. I may have to shut down for a few days, actually. To tell you the truth, I feel sick."

"But this is crazy, Herbert! I mean who—why would they?"

"Vengeance? A competitor? An outright nut? All morning long I've been asking myself. Could it have been a drug theft? No, because none was taken. A robbery? But there's no cash here to steal. There are a couple of other possibilities, including a rival named Melman, and a patient or two who owes me money. And I'm sure I've accumulated my share of enemies in life. But this . . . I mean the nastiness of it!" Minkoff's voice began to rise. "The goddamned craziness! Lunacy! I mean we're talking savages! Madmen!"

Harta said nothing, and after a few seconds, the doctor, panting, composed himself and said in a low voice, "Sorry, but the whole thing has bent me completely out of whack. You know my collection of Benin statuary?"

"They didn't!"

"Yes, they did, I'm afraid. Broken into little bits and pieces."

"Migod, Herbert, I could get frightened if I let myself."

"I could get a gun," he said grimly, "and break a few

skulls if I let myself. But I can promise you one thing, when we catch the persons responsible, they won't be sent, they'll be *flown* up the river."

"Well, that's good. Are there clues of any sort?"

"No suspects, but a clear fingerprint."

I felt a blinding white flash of light, followed by the sensation of lifting sickeningly out of my body.

"Mmm," said Harta, not listening too closely, "great. But you sound so tense, you poor dear. I think you could use a little TLC, eh?"

There was a pause.

"I bet I know how to make you forget that break-in," said Harta softly.

Another long pause. Was Minkoff switching phones?

"I bet you could," said Minkoff, more gently. "And I bet I'm willing. I should have my composure back by then, at least. Dear God what a morning! And now I've gotta fly—the detective's here."

"Soon, then," said Harta.

"Very," said Minkoff, and hung up with a lengthy kissing noise.

There was a silence, and then I heard her feet on the stairs taking light, quick, happy steps. I dialed Derwent with violent pulls of the index finger.

"A fingerprint," I hissed when he answered.

"What? Who is this?"

"It's me, Derwent."

"Denny?"

"They found one, Derwent."

"Who did?"

"The cops, at Minkoff's."

"Are you serious?"

"Yeah, I just heard it on the phone."

Silence lay on the line, a long moment of absolute silence.

"Well?" I said, "I was supposed to 'leave it all to you.' Now what, huh, you stupid jerk?"

The silence continued, broken abruptly by what I took to be a door slamming open and shut six times, with a sound like gunshots. When Derwent got back on the phone, breathing hard, he said that "after mature consideration," he'd realized the fingerprint must be mine, because he'd "wiped everywhere he shat." He added that "for obvious prophylactic reasons" he thought it would be best if we didn't see each other again for several months, and hung up. I sat listening to the radiant vacancy of the dial tone for a moment, disappointed in Derwent's lack of nerve for the first time in my life, and then I slowly put the phone back in the cradle.

TWENTY-TWO

Before anything else could happen, school began. It began as the Yankees fell to next-to-last place in the American League and the war in Vietnam widened on television like a great dark bird opening its wings. A "massive escalation" of the war was in progress in early September, an escalation that Max, in a rare outburst, angrily described at the breakfast table one morning as a "genocide." In the midst of constant coverage of the "call-up of troops," of soldiers swinging smartly onto trucks and planes and trains and mothers bidding good-bye with waving hankies, school began gradually, almost unannounced, like somebody sneaking up on you from behind and blowing breath on your neck.

Usually, school began amid an avalanche of *things*. The year before Harta had taken me to Salzinger's Stationery for little zipper bags, fresh notebooks, and the luxury of sunny sharp pencils and pink erasers that reminded me of flesh. She had bought me new corduroys and a sailor shirt and sat me down and given me a pep talk, holding my shoulder blades with lightly pinching fingers and lecturing me on my responsibilities for the upcoming year in a special songlike voice that was used, like her best china, only for fancy occasions.

This year, there were no new clothes, no pencils, no protractors or rulers—nothing, in fact, other than a quick, deep hug on the first day of classes. And though I wanted to do something dramatic, to complain passionately, to fall to one knee and plead my case in a rush of hot words, I knew it would be no use. Harta, it was clear, was simply far too involved with her doctor and the upcoming exam with Fad to pay much attention to the start of the school year. Max was bitterly withdrawn, and said nothing at all. So, for the most part quietly, sulking slightly, I started school.

School again: flat, echoing, loud voices in the corridors, shrieks of recognition after summer vacation, endless click and scrawl of chalk on the board, and attached to the chalk, at the head of the class, a bottle-shaped homeroom teacher named Miss Sundifen, with a fixed smile on her face, posing like an illustration in an old book under the word *Fierce*. She put her hands on her hips. This year, she said, will under no circumstances be like the last. This year, my dears, we will *work*. Outside the classroom windows, the sun was floating in the sky looking the same as ever, but taking something with it each day, some heated piece of summer that never came back. Mrs. Sundifen said, I'm very pleased to welcome you back to class—girls, no lipstick; boys, no hats. I won't even mention high heels and T-shirts. Now, so that we can better get to know one another, I would like us to write a paper on what we did with our summers. Be honest, be candid, and be kind. Remember that even the things that seem most obvious and boring to you can be interesting to someone else who is from another family, with another background. Before we begin writing, however, I have an important question to ask: Denny Graubart, *where are your pants?*

I sat up in bed with a start, the sounds of hooting laughter dying in my ears. Waves of gratefulness washed over me as I felt the familiar relief: *It was only a dream*. And yet, for the millionth time, I had forgotten.

What, just now, lying in bed, was I importantly forgetting?

I got up, and noticed the contents of my room seeming to ripple with a kind of freshness. Then I remembered: Today was the Event. The trip to Trenton for the Comprehensive Exam. I got dressed and padded downstairs and into the kitchen, where I found Harta alone in her quilted bathrobe, wheeling to and fro in busy little arcs as she laid out the grapefruits and cereal bowls, napkins and silverware, and lit the flame with a small thump of ignition under the coffee. She paused in midspin, greeted me with a smile, and then, as if I didn't know already, as if what I'd calculated to be two hundred home sessions hadn't been secretly building to this moment in time, she began explaining to me just how important this day was going to be to our family, all the while continuing to repeat the words "direct bearing." The Comprehensive Exam had a "direct bearing" on our family's future together. And more importantly, my own behavior would have a "direct bearing" on the way things went at the exam.

"Yes," said Harta, putting up her hands as if to forestall criticism, "*your* behavior. You should feel honored," she said, "because the doctors will be talking not only to James but to you, too, at length." She stabbed a small knife into the bloodshot pink eye of a grapefruit, began scoring radial lines. "And you're to say whatever comes into your mind. Do you understand? Whatever. For example, you might explain to them how much James has meant to you, and how he brings out the best in all of us. We're a regular family, happy and healthy, just like everyone else, and that's what you should tell them, okay?" Her voice was rising. "You have to tell them that, okay? It's in fact absolutely, critically important. It will have a direct bear—" She stopped a moment, breathing hard. Max and Fad were entering the kitchen. In a composed, gentle voice she said, "Darling, I'm sure you'll just be yourself."

After a quiet breakfast, we got dressed in the unaccustomed stiffness of our fancy clothes. Fad wore his new suit from Duboff's, while I had on something that Harta picked out for me from Fad's old rejects. The pants seemed to bind and catch, and I felt the jacket pulling hard under the arms, but I didn't care. Max was wearing his blue suit with the neck open. But Harta—Harta was dressed like a queen, an actual queen come out to walk among her subjects. Overlapping filmy scales dripped from her body. Knifelike high heels raised her height. She had on a new watch and a necklace of gold chains with a green stone held in a little metal claw at the center and she had done what she described to Maude as "a Parisian thing" with her hair, which had been whipped up all over her head like a large, dark meringue.

We tramped out of the house to join Max, who was already sitting waiting for us in the idling Impala, two fangs of smoke stabbing the air from the dual exhausts. The Impala was a big, very fast car, for which Max had ordered a "performance option." This meant that the engine, when Max revved it, roared with the exact sound of a crowd at a football game. Clambering into the car, we left at ten on the dot, and within minutes of departure the interstate picked us up and began carrying us south at speed. Green highway signs bulleted by overhead for NEWARK, WESTFIELD, SHORE POINTS, and NEW BRUNSWICK, each of them dwindling dimensionally perfect in the rearview mirror. Landscape ran alongside the car in a mix of shiny diners, truckyards, warehouses, golf courses and the colored mystic symbols displayed high over gas stations, which seemed to state specific reasons to swerve off the road and fill your tank. You would float like a winged horse, burst like a glowing star, or if you went to Esso you would be cool and placid and ovally at your ease.

"So," said Harta, exhaling in a long, deep, endless breath, "who's for an apple?" She had turned around to us and was smiling brightly. I ignored her completely as Fad sat rigid, twittering, and Max, dead silent, drove. "C'mon, everybody," she said. "What's with all the long faces, eh? Let's relax already and have a bite!" Out of the corner of my eye, I watched as her smile slowly wilted, and her hands dropped. When she finally turned back around to the front, I leaned forward, stared a moment at the back of her head where a patch of pink scalp peeked through, silently made the face for "gross," and then turned away. After an hour and a half on the highway, we pulled off and into the city of Trenton, where we navigated the busy side streets for a few minutes and finally arrived at our destination: an office tower that looked like a giant grandfather clock. Where the six would be on the clock face there was a garage entrance, giving way to a banked spiral drive, which carried us several hundred feet below the earth and ended, abruptly, in a giant painting of an open hand with the word STOP! lettered across its palm. We left the car with the attendant, got on a nearby elevator, and rocketed upward for what felt like a hundred floors before emerging finally onto a quiet carpeted aisle, where a scatter of staff people, dressed all in white, seemed to turn together and stare at us in surprise.

"The Graubart family?" said a nurse, coming toward us, smiling. We followed her through a door and down a hallway that was long and dead-white with fluorescent overhead lights. She motioned us into another room and we sat. The door closed behind the nurse with a sigh.

"Mommy?" asked Fad in a low voice, nearly a whisper.

"Yes?" Harta was not only heavily made up, but perfumed, I observed. I liked the scent, but was unable to remember its name.

"When Daddy hit me two years ago yesterday why didn't he go away?" Max snorted loudly as Harta bent forward and began frantically smoothing the collar of Fad's shirt, saying, "I don't remember, and anyway, don't dwell on the negative. Remember our saying?"

"No, Mommy."

"When in doubt, never shout. When feeling bad, head for glad."

"I think I have to go to the bathroom," said Fad.

She shot to her feet, wobbled a second on her heels, breasts waving as if to signal HELP! and then grabbed him by the arm, pulling him from the room so fast he almost left the ground. In the ensuing silence, Max and I were left alone. An air-conditioning unit purred quietly. I looked at Max. He was staring out the window, bathed in high-altitude sunlight that, as it touched the far side of his face, made it look like half his head was missing.

He shot his index finger up in the air.

"I'll be right back," he said.

He returned a minute later, accompanied by a distinctive smell—that familiar fruity, yeasty odor of whiskey. I had seen no pocket flask beneath his clothes on the way here; nonetheless he must have hidden one somewhere. But Max, meanwhile, was sitting back down, staring out the window, getting ready, I could tell by the many small movements of his head, to speak.

"There it is, kiddo," he said, staring out the window.

I looked, saw nothing special.

"What, Dad?"

"The world, son. You think it's easy? It's as hard as hard can be. They let you stay in it just long enough so that you begin to get really good at it, and then they come"—his voice drifted downward—"and they take it all away from you."

"What do you mean, Dad?"

"What do I mean? I mean they grind you down, is what. Day in day out they work on you, until you're just another expendable little thing, a broken pencil that wears a hat."

"Who does, Dad?" I had no idea what he was talking about and yet at the same time was terrified that I might miss something.

"Are you kidding? The question is who doesn't. Your friends, your parents, your wife, your in-laws. They get right inside your head and they say, Go for it—you, with the shining eyes. Reach for the stars! Knock the world flat! Make a big impression! You know what that translates to? A thirty-year mortgage, a wife who isn't in the mood, a yard with a tree in it, and a vacation once a year to some filthy island where they serve this absolute dreck for food that—but Christ what am I saying?" He shook his head as if to clear it. "You're just a kid. Come here." I took two steps toward him on the springy carpet, and when I drew near he gathered me in a headlock and mussed my hair.

"Big shot," he whispered. "High roller. World-beater. Your old man can still dust your skull, can't he?"

It was our phrase for that time, usually on major holidays, when he got so drunk he became helplessly friendly. Somehow all of this was wrong at the moment. Nonetheless, I said, "Sure, Dad," and squeezed out a laugh.

He smoothed down my hair and drew his hands along my cheek. His touch was weirdly electric, and for one shocking moment I thought he was going to kiss me.

"I think what I'm trying to say is we have to talk," said Max.

"What about?"

"Well, I've decided that I want you to know—" He stopped.

"What, Dad?"

"That sometimes things aren't what they seem—"

"What kind of things?"

"Between men and women, Denny." He looked up at me, blinking as if trying to connect my face to someone he knew. "You see," he went on, "it's nice to think that life is like a little equation in math, and that if you put the right number in one end, the right result will come out the other. But son, it doesn't work like that."

"It doesn't?"

"You've got to be flexible," Max said, as if talking partially to himself. "You've got to adapt, or you die like the dinosaurs."

There was a long pause. Max rolled his eyes up until they met mine.

"What do you say to that, eh?"

I felt the ground shift under my feet.

"That's—" I stuttered, "that's—"

Max smiled sadly.

"That's *life*, is the word you're looking for, sonny," he said. "The Big Chance. The thing that never waits up for you. The one and only." Max was on some strange tear I'd never heard before. Did he know about Harta? He continued nodding his head. "When I was your age, I thought everything about grown-up life was like furniture—solid, heavy, and forever and ever. I thought adults lived in a world of statues, and nothing ever changed. Hoo-boy, was I wrong!"

Reaching under his suit jacket, he withdrew the beautiful silver pocket flask and took a long swallow.

"Mommy said you're not supposed to drink in public," I said, unable to help myself.

ELI GOTTLIEB

"Shut your ass," said Max affectionately, knocking back another long, swilling gulp. He sighed loudly, and then replaced the flask.

"And what happens when you get older," he said, picking up the thread again, "is it all begins to vibrate fast, life. It's not composed of anything stable at all. It just looks that way to kids. In fact it's shaking so fast you can't believe it, Den. Like in a rodeo ride or something. How to get off, where to go—you don't know! It's just whoo-ee, hang on tight! And the older you get the faster it all happens. *It* moves, not you. *It*. And it roars, too. You can hear it, if you listen hard. Like the sound of the ocean in a shell. But louder. The months just whipping past, faster and faster. And then you turn over in bed, and it's a new year. You take the stairs of your house, and Jesuschrist, by the time you get to the top—it's a new year! You can't slow down, you get me? Even if you want to catch your breath, see the sights, take the slow boat, you gotta hop. You gotta sprint. You gotta run for your life. And maybe, one day, you sit up and realize that *is* your life, the running. That's mainly what you've been doing all along. Catch my drift?"

"Dad?" I said.

"What, son?"

I looked at him, smiling widely. "Dad, you're talking!"

Max smiled himself, leaning back against the cushions as the door flew open and Harta and Fad burst into the room, panting.

"Has the doctor come yet?" she asked, breathless.

"Nobody here but us ghosts," said Max, his smile fading as he turned away from her to the window and stared out at the city.

Harta pulled Fad down onto the couch next to her and began whispering something to him. Whatever it was, it caused him to laugh delightedly, and cry, "Really, Mommy? Really?"

"Yes," said Harta proudly, "it works like that every time." She was nodding her head in agreement with herself. "It's what we call a sure thing."

The door opened and the nurse leaned forward into the room at the angle of an alpine ski jumper.

"We're ready," she said simply.

Harta again hauled Fad to his feet, and vanished with the nurse. In the silence, Max began humming something, a tune of mournful longing that seemed vaguely familiar. He took another belt from his flask, and belched discreetly. To the window, he said, "There are many ways to deal with it—I mean the nastiness, the stick-it-in-your-eye disappointments of life. Some people jump out windows. Some become obsessed with being business big shots. Some lose themselves in drugs and things like that, or go to monasteries or get strokes at a young age. Others," Max, sighing, said to the window, "get married."

The door glided open.

"Lunch call!" Harta cried, reentering the room at a brisk saunter, radiantly confident. "The Graubarts have officially been given license to kill two hours."

We took the same pinging elevator down to street level, and exited into hard, flat city light. "Where should we go for eats?" Harta asked Max, but he shook his head, grimly, and walked straight ahead. "I guess that means right here!" Harta shouted after him, pausing in front of the familiar bright orange façade of a Howard Johnson's. She opened the door and I walked in, followed by Max, who was staring at the ground with his hands in his pockets. The hostess found us a seat at the back, near the kitchen, where an odor of tired food quickly settled over us. The restaurant was jammed. Heavy laminated menus were soon placed in our hands. These were filled with photographs of fantastic rainbow-colored entrées and appetizers piled in shapes that resembled the temples of a lost civilization. I ordered fried clams and "freshly squozen orange juice" and kept my eyes on the food for the rest of lunch. Harta chirped away brightly, exclaiming over how nice and efficient and intelligent the Trenton Mental Health people were, and how she was sure everything would turn out all right. Max, I noticed, said nothing at all, and continued humming a sad melody to himself.

Lunch over, we walked in a tight group back to the office building, again rocketed upward in the pinging elevator, and strolled back to our waiting room. As we sat back in our chairs, Max excused himself, saying he was going outside to smoke a cigar. Harta gave him a look of slashing quick disapproval, but he ignored it, and left the room.

She placed her hands over her head and stretched with a big sigh. I heard joints cracking. Her hands fell back into her lap.

"How you doing in the middle of all this, honeybunch?" she asked.

"Fine, Ma."

"I'm so proud of you." She reached over and grabbed my hand, but I jerked it away.

"I understand," she said, nodding. "You're angry. Who wouldn't be in your situation? All I can say is, no matter how bad you think you have it, just remember your brother has it worse. To have all those gifts and be unable to express them." She shook her head slowly from side to side to show regret.

"The musical ear, the sensitivity, the way with certain— certain concepts. *You* know what I'm talking about, don't you, sweetheart?"

I said nothing.

"Remember the time we went to that concert for kids and the conductor asked anyone in the crowd to identify the piece of music that had just been played, and your brother, he didn't even raise his hand, he just blurted it out, the entire title—and the only one in the room to get it?"

"No."

"There's a word people use when they talk about coal, trees, things like that. The word is *underutilized*. You remember that word because that's what your brother is—not retarded, but underutilized."

She was talking extra loud and very distinctly. I noticed that her smile was unnaturally bright and her eyes were snapping.

She tapped her temple.

"*I* knew," she said, "from the moment I pressed the keys on the piano and watched those eyes fly open and that little rosebud mouth draw up in a smile so bright, so beautiful, it would break your heart—did I know? You bet! This was special, like no one had seen for years. And I know from music, it's my passion, darling. The ear, the memory for notes and phrases, it's something that can't be taught. Once in a generation, a Rubinstein, a Horowitz. And it happened to my own *yingele*."

"Ma, can I go to the bathroom?"

She sat bolt upright. "Can you—do you know where it is?"

"Down the hall, right?"

Slowly, she relaxed again. "Yeah, make a left out the door."

I entered a space that was so perfectly clean and white it seemed carved out of a block of soap. The only sound was the faint buzz of the fluorescent lighting, which the bareness of the room seemed to magnify. Rows of urinals like undershot jaws ran down one wall. As I walked over to one, I stopped, arrested by my reflection in the gigantic mirror. I stood there a moment calmly, and then lunged swiftly forward and, freezing myself an inch away, beheld . . . nothing. If I got it just right I saw a space, a lashed void where my eyes had been, a shimmery vacancy that seemed to radiate outward in straight lines from my pupil and turn me as perfectly, effortlessly hollow as a balloon.

I toyed with the sensation, lunging close, pulling slowly back. On occasion, cutting my eyes sideways toward the mirror, I could make out a trail of sorts, a small, slow-traveling echo of my body as it crossed from inside my head to that other world of coffeepots, car windows, knives, and still water that shone so brilliantly with my reflected self.

As the day dragged on, I found myself spending a lot of time at Mirror Games. There was very little else to do. I drank water, drained it, lunged listlessly forward and back and paced the corridors. It seemed late in the afternoon by the time the door to the waiting room swung open and Fad came out, looking pale and distracted and staring at the ground. He was accompanied by a nurse who seemed to be eyeing him warily as she walked him to the seat near us, sat him down, then walked away without saying another thing.

Harta leaned over and grabbed him on either side of the face.

"Welcome back from the war. How'd it go, yum-yum?"

"Maybe bad," said Fad. "Maybe not so good."

"What do you mean, James?" Harta had reared back a few inches. Max, returned earlier, now leaned forward with an expression I believed to be encouragement. I sat watching.

"I got volts," he said. Harta slumped. "Volts" was the code for when Fad felt invaded by angry electricity, barbed and shooting transmissions of power that came into his body and caused him to scream, flail his arms about, jump up and down, fling things, and sink his teeth into his hand. I stole a look at his hand. Sure enough, spittle glistened on the freshly bitten web between thumb and forefinger.

"A lot of volts?" Harta asked in a small voice.

"Lots and lots."

The door opened and the doctor appeared, frowning. He was a short, round-shouldered man with a whitish smock and a look of sustained exposure to fluorescent lighting.

"Mrs. Graubart."

"Of course!" Harta cried, too loudly, far too loudly, and jumped to her feet, towering over the little man. He nodded, merely, and held the door for her as she barreled by him and into the hall.

I turned to look at Fad, who was as flat-out far away as he could get at that moment. He was chittering at high speed, but without any happiness, it seemed to me. Max had turned around and was staring back out the window at the city below, his head tilted against the glass.

"Denny?" Fad asked.

"What?"

"Am I going away now?"

"I don't know, Fad."

"But Denny, I don't want to go away. Can't I stay at home like you and I'll be a nice boy?"

"I said I don't know!"

Ten minutes later Harta came back, looking—well, looking terrible. Her face was dull and flat and her eyes were small. She was bending slightly forward as she walked, trying, it seemed, to control a bad stomachache.

"Let's go," she said simply, avoiding our gazes.

"But Mom?" I asked. "I thought I was going to see the doctor, too." After all this time, I wanted my moment.

"Let's go *now!*" she said fiercely, raising her eyes to me. They were wet with tears.

Silently we rode down in the elevator. Wordless, we drove the hour and a half home. We would, Max told me later that day, his arm around my shoulder, flask-breath in my face, be officially notified by mail.

TWENTY-THREE

Mrs. Sundifen leaned forward and put her weight on her knuckles. Then she pursed her lips, and pointed dramatically back over her shoulder at the blackboard, where the word *Mesozoic* was written in flowing letters. "What do we know of the Mesozoic?" she asked. No one said a thing. Mrs. Sundifen frowned, and began to talk with the special voice she used when lecturing, three parts air to one part sound, that always gave the impression of a very thin string of water falling on a rock. A wave of sleep rolled through me. Mrs. Sundifen was explaining that the Mesozoic was a period in geologic time that was the age of the great reptiles. It was the very moment, she added, when big-finned dinosaurs first crawled out of the hot broth of early life, put a foot on land, and began gradually flaking away in the infinite winds of time, losing their teeth and their impaling talons and their general terribleness until they reached the final evolutionary stage of—of what? she asked.

I looked around me groggily. Everyone was staring at each other.

"Of us!" Mrs. Sundifen said. "Of you and me." Mrs. Sundifen seemed very pleased with this explanation, and smiled and clapped her hands together for a moment, before coughing and turning to write another word on the board. She was just writing the word *saber-tooth* when the bell rang for the end of class, and kept on ringing as I scooped my books into my book bag and left the classroom to go home.

As I walked back up the hill to our house, I saw the mailman several houses below ours, and I put on a burst of speed. I arrived at our house just before he did, and stood on the lawn, where I took the mail from his hand with a friendly nod. Among the handbills and advertising circulars was a long, knife-thin envelope with the state seal on one end and lots of fancy spit-curled lettering clustering around it. Everything about the envelope screamed Famous! Important! Dangerous! Clearly, it was from the Trenton state commissioner's office. I entered the house quietly, made certain Harta was upstairs, and then steamed the letter open, as usual, over the teakettle. The writer began by clearing his throat with words like "intractable schizophrenic tendencies, complicated by obsessional anxiety," and then he got down to business. "Due to unforeseen results obtained in the opening diagnostic evaluations," he wrote, "fiscal monies formerly earmarked for the rehabilitation of James Graubart are from this date on rescinded." I didn't understand all the words, but I got the general idea: case closed, and bye-bye brother. Resealing the letter, I replaced it in the box, and soon after, heard the squeak of the mailbox being opened again by Harta, and, thirty seconds later, a gasp, followed by the clubbing sounds of her feet on the stairs. I slipped down to my basement extension, and when I picked up the receiver heard her voice, on the phone to Maude, sprinting, falling, stumbling forward wildly. "They've done it!" she shouted. "They threw the switch! It's over! Ten thousand pipe-smoking idiots in the state offices at Trenton," she wailed, "and I can't save a single deserving child!" She hung up, after refusing Maude's offer of "what we call, like, a major drink," and jumped hurriedly in her car. Without even saying good-bye to me, she zoomed out of the driveway, and then in a threshing of gears, screeched the tires as she left.

I spent the afternoon idly reviewing my notes, and two hours later, Harta returned, looking much, much calmer. When I asked her where she'd been, she ignored me and explained, somewhat fake-cheerily, that she and my father had decided to have our first ever "family meeting" that night, after dinner. I tried to catch her eye and hold it, but she turned away, went to her bedroom, shut the door, and stayed there, silent.

For dinner that night, Harta served Swanson fried chicken TV dinners, which I loved because they tasted great and allowed me to pretend that we were sitting in an airplane eating dinner while taxiing for takeoff. I made a variety of propeller noises while eating, but nobody seemed to notice. Harta was very nervous and kept getting up from the table for napkins and useless extra spoons and forks. Fad rocked and moaned to himself, and Max, as usual, drank lots of beer and said nothing at all.

As soon as dinner was over, we met in the "music room"—a dim, carpeted space where the Steinway grand piano crouched like the polished coffin for a huge french curve. On the wall were Harta's favorite reproductions of Chagall and Picasso, along with paintings on wood of ancient Greeks, who carried the tubby guitars called lyres and danced with mournfully inert expressions on their faces. Candles burned. We sat in a semicircle, Harta at the center.

She cleared her throat, straightened up, and then tilted forward slightly.

"There is no easy way to begin what I have to say, so I

might as well just jump in. I've asked that we gather here tonight because James, we've just found out, is going off to Ramphill Village next week. He's doing this because very powerful people who work for the state of New Jersey think it would be the best thing for him. But what I want you to know is *it's not forever*. It's just, in fact, until we figure out what to do next." Harta pronounced these words very carefully, sending them out through all the upward-straining muscles of her face. It was not a smile, exactly.

Fad made a noise.

"Look," she said, waving her hands, "we're just trying this thing out, is the point. We'll have another family conference just like this, in a couple of months, at Ramphill Village, and you'll see if you like it there, and if you don't, darling"— she lowered her hands to her thighs and took a deep breath— "maybe we'll just take you back home or we'll find another place."

"Okay?" she asked. I looked up into her face again. It was devoid of makeup, and all the crying she'd done since receiving the letter that morning had given her a pink, swollen look that actually made her seem youthful, after a fashion.

"Okay?" she said, this time a little less firmly. "I want you to know"—she raised her eyes to include the rest of us— "I want all of you to know, that I think everybody has tried very very hard, and no one should in any way feel bad about what's happening. In a very real way, it's for the best."

"Mwahhhh," Fad said.

"Now," she said, "I don't have to remind anyone how important family life is, but in keeping with the occasion, I've decided to read a poem I've written over these last difficult few days. It's for all of us really."

She looked around at us, one by one, took out a small

notebook, cleared her throat, and then in a voice so slow she seemed hypnotized, she read:

> The family is like an endless road
> That people, verily, must travel
> And though they carry a heavy load
> And though they feel their lives unravel
> Betimes the family buoys them up
> And keeps them smiling ever bright
> For when deep stress and darkness strike
> They know where to turn to find a light.

Harta paused, looked around bright-eyed, and then went on:

> And when in a family a certain soul
> Decides to strike out on his own
> And goes away to a sunny place
> Where flowers bloom and milk cows moan
> And the people laugh and love each other right
> Then his family is happy and its heart is light
> So go in peace my darling child
> And remember if ever things look black
> Just call your Mommy, who'll come fast in her car
> And write endless words on your back!

There was a silence, during which Harta sat for a moment staring down at the page and clenching and unclenching her fists, as if trying to recover her self-control. I sat smiling faintly, having no idea of what she'd just said, though I perceived its odd, pounding rhythm, like a cheerleading chant at a football game. Fad, a million miles away, stared into space.

"Nice language," said Max. "But then again you were always a good writer."

Harta smiled.

"It's just too bad," said Max, "that your fancy sentiments about our family seem so selectively applied."

The curve of her smile fell flat. "Excuse me?" she said.

"Oh, nothing," said Max, "nothing at all." Something in his tone alerted me and I looked closer, taking in the eyes and the looseness around the mouth. Max was drunk.

"No please," said Harta, staring at him oddly, "go ahead."

"No, no, I don't want to interrupt this beautiful"—he paused a long time on the word—"little ritual you planned for your family. I love when you do the hearts and flowers stuff, Harta, just love it to death. It's so sincere, isn't it? I mean you put so much of yourself into it. And we know what it comes from, at bottom. It comes from your deep love of your family, doesn't it? Of course it does!"

"What are you doing? I mean *what are you doing?*" Harta cried, glaring at him. "For months you walk around the house deaf and dumb, with a face on you like you're having horrible indigestion. And now you come home in the state you're in and interrupt a beautiful moment with this kind of garbage?"

Max began to speak, but Harta cut him off. "It would be different," she said, "if we had had a fair distribution of responsibilities around the house. But excuse me if I don't remember it quite that way. Let me put it to you plain, my husband: For fourteen years it's been me who schlepped to and fro, me who kept the records, me who sacrificed my every waking hour to the maintenance and improvement of this family, and in particular our eldest son. And for what I've done, and my years of struggle, I get you"—she flicked her hands as if to make him go away—"saying these crazy terrible things about me, and doing it in front of the children no less?"

I swiveled my gaze to Max. Off to one side, I could see Fad rocking excitedly. Vaguely, I heard a car pull up outside, but ignored it. Max leaned forward, and to my amazement, he smiled.

"Why are you getting so hot under the collar, Harta? I'm saying only what eyes can see and ears can hear: that you've been a wonderful wife to our family. Of course, if you've gone to new lengths to define the concept of family, that's all right, isn't it? I mean I should feel honored to have a what—brother-in-law, husband-in-law?—who's a doctor, right? A doctor in the family!"

Harta sighed gigantically. "You know," she said softly, "right here"—she put her hand on her heart—"I have a pain so large it could explode me maybe into little pieces. After all this time together, that you could possibly read me as wrong as what you just said—I mean, it makes me want to just run away and swear off ever speaking another word to a soul again in my life!"

Max stroked his mouth with the fingers of a hand. He pursed his lips. "Really? Are you sure?"

The doorbell rang. Harta got up to get it.

"You get me so crazy at times!" she said in a furious lowered voice as she walked across the room. "On top of everything else, you've simply destroyed this beautiful occasion. All I needed was a few hours of your cooperation to make everything graceful and nice. The little things in life, remember?"

Harta composed her face and opened the door. A second later, drawing a deep breath, she gasped. Into the house, bowing and nodding, walked the small, wild-haired figure of Dr. Minkoff.

"Good day, all," said the doctor in a wavering voice. "I know, I know." He raised his hands on either side of his head.

"What am I doing here, right? I don't normally make house calls. But your husband, Mrs. Graubart, is an exceedingly persuasive man."

"The who, how then—" said Harta indistinctly, slumping back against the wall.

"My wife," said Max, "is a little less than perfectly articulate at the moment. Aren't you, darling?"

Harta opened her mouth and drew breath as if to speak. And then she merely held her mouth open, looking as surprised as I was.

"I have come to talk to you because your husband and I discussed things at length," said Minkoff, who looked ill, I thought, "and he was worried about the way you would take this apparent setback. We decided that, seeing as I've had a—a bearing on the case, I should reassure you that you've done everything a person could be expected to do. I know that I brought you along, hoping for the best, and none of this was fraudulent, Mrs. Graubart. It was real on my part. There really was hope. As there is with all children of James's type and degree of disorder. It's a crap shoot, and you have lost this round. But rest assured, there are many more rounds to go."

Harta leaned forward, her mouth still open.

"Oh, many, many more," said the gray, perspiring Dr. Minkoff.

Max sat back against the couch, crossed his arms on his chest, and smiled widely. "You see, Harta," he said, "the good old doc here says there are many more rounds to go. What do you think of that, eh?"

Harta turned to look at Max, entirely ignoring Minkoff.

"Your husband was very concerned about you, Mrs. Graubart," said Minkoff, to the back of her head. "You should know that. *Very* concerned."

Harta continued to ignore the doctor, who abruptly put

a fist in front of his mouth, like he was going to cough. But he didn't cough.

She shook her head, as if in disbelief.

"You're playing a game, Max Graubart," she said slowly, "a very dangerous and poisonous game. Did you think I would shrivel up and die? I'm not scared of you. I'm appalled that you did this in front of the children. But that's okay. They'll live. As will I." She took a deep breath. "What I've done in life I've done because I had to survive as a feeling human being."

Harta had been talking like someone addressing a large crowd. But as soon as she finished speaking, she seemed to slump, as if suddenly exhausted. She turned slowly to Minkoff.

"Thank you for coming," she said in a diminished voice. "We've all been a bit ill, but a house call was not necessary." She looked at us, one by one. "Excuse me, all," she said dully. "I'm very tired, and very unhappy. I'm going to sleep."

Staring at no one, wobbling as if slightly drunk, she walked slowly out of the room. We all sat there listening to her take the stairs, and then, almost inaudibly, the bedroom door click shut.

TWENTY-FOUR

Minkoff was helped back into his car by Max, who to my utter astonishment put his arm around him as he walked him across the lawn. When Max came back in, his face was spilled strangely off to one side, and he strode right past us as if we didn't exist, and marched straight upstairs. "Did Mommy and Daddy have a fight?" Fad asked, but I ignored him, went upstairs myself, lay in bed, and thought that if I lived to be a hundred years old, I would never understand the ways of grown-ups. More than ever, it was clear that adults were a race apart, grown up in another country and speaking our language only by a freak accident of human science. I mean (I told myself, lying with my sleepless head on the hot pillow) I had seen Max's life insurance forms, and knew he weighed over 200 pounds. Why, therefore, hadn't he beaten the crap out of shrimpy Minkoff? Why hadn't he taken out a pistol and blown his brains back to Bloomfield? Was it because Max was a Marxist, possibly? Was it because he was dedicated to "universal literacy" and "workers' rights" that he allowed a pudgy guy to touch his wife in the secret center of her body, and then (I couldn't get over this) put his arm around him as he walked him to his car?

I finally drifted off to sleep, but it was a bad sleep, and I woke up with a feeling of having been deeply, wordlessly cheated in life. When I went downstairs, I found Max alone in the kitchen, thawing out a mountain of frozen food and avoiding my eye. Out the side of his mouth he explained that he and Harta were "working something out," but that it didn't "concern a couple of real sluggers like your brother and yourself." And although I wanted more than anything else in the world at that moment to shout loud, specific, and angry words at my father, I kept my mouth shut and my feelings to myself.

For the entire next day and a half of the weekend, Harta remained a ghost around the house. She stayed locked in the bedroom with Max, from where I occasionally heard the shower running, the toilet flushing, and their voices making soft, lulling sounds, hers sometimes breaking upward and being caught by his and brought gently back down, his rising in sharp, repetitive sounds of what I took to be accusation. Twice a day, Max brought another defrosted plate of food up to Harta. Once, I heard them watch the nightly news. I kept to myself, and faintly enjoyed the strange energy coming out of my parents' bedroom, which reminded me of being around a cage of trapped birds.

I was tempted to call friends, but didn't. I tried to read novels, but couldn't get far. Mostly I scanned my notebooks, trying to put some shape into this very strange summer, and did scattered background study on my report on *Tyrannosaurus rex* for school. Fad, when I saw him, acted like nothing at all was about to happen to him, or if it was, he didn't care. An entire slow day and night drifted by like this. Finally, on Sunday afternoon, while lying on my bed, I heard her bedroom door creak open and her voice say something, and I scooted out to see. To my astonishment, Max and Harta, fully dressed, freshly made up and perfumed, were holding hands! With a strange, shy look on their faces I'd never seen before, they announced that they were going out to dinner, and could we mind the store?

Dinner? Now? Now, when a thunder clap should have burst from the bedroom and shivered the house to bits? Now, when Harta and Max should have rolled out the front door and down the hill in a ball of punching arms and legs? Where was the cataclysm? Where the sirens? "Oh, and Denny," Harta, added, smiling as she handed me a piece of paper with the name and phone of the restaurant scribbled on it, "do you think you could whip up some Chef Boyardee for your brother and yourself?"

A new chapter had been abruptly opened in the book of that summer, a mysterious chapter entitled "How Happy We Are," starring the momentarily upset and now blazingly happy Harta Graubart, and her sidekick, Max. Something deep and weird had happened to my parents, and I wasn't sure I liked it. I had been so careful over the last few months, attending to tiny signs of change, keeping records of charts of trends and recurrences, attempting, in a variety of ways, to draw up the big picture. And now this sudden eruption of parental cheer like a bomb going off—it unnerved me. In the end, however, I had little choice in the matter. A command had been issued in veiled language from my parents, and that command was: Be happy, or else.

Over the next few days, as I sat in my room collecting information on teeth and jaws of the dinosaurs of the Late Cretaceous period, I watched, passively, as if from the bleacher seats, the new electricity that seemed to be sizzling through my family. Harta was in constant motion, a whirl-wind of cheer whom I watched zoom to and fro, packing Fad's records and shoes, boxing his toiletries, sorting and ironing his clothes at speed. It was seemingly the height of fun for her to sew labels into all his waistbands and collars, whistling and making jokes as she did so. It was deeply pleasant for her to head out to J. J. Newberrys to shop for his combs and brushes and candy-smelling shampoos. It was a treat to spend hours a day locked in conversation with the "transition specialist" from Ramphill Village, a woman named Mrs. Benson, who spoke as through a pencil sharpener that turned all her speech into impaling pointy phrases. In Mrs. Benson's words, it was important that Harta understand the "psychoemotive implications of departure," and the "disequilibriums that attach to change for the developmentally disabled."

Yes, said Harta, yes, of course.

The only flaw in the happy picture Harta was trying to paint of our home was Fad himself. Not that he exploded. No, he threw no scenes, had no tantrums. He instead went deep inside himself, to some spooky, far-off alcove of the mind whose gravity was too dense to permit the birth of words. Sitting silent at the dinner table, silent on the living room couch as Harta played his favorite, Stravinsky's "Firebird," on the piano; silently dragging himself to and fro around the house, he wore at all times in those last days an air-cloak of heavy despair that caused his shoulders to round, his posture to grow even more stooped. Occasionally, in response to direct questions, he moved his mouth inaudibly, shifting the strange diagonal line across his face from one side to the other.

Harta tried to bring her cheer into his life. She spent lots of time with him in his room, talking, laughing, and joking, her voice coming through the closet in warm, familiar waves. She took him on the local commuter train, which he usually loved. She drew an entire dictionary of words on his back. But Fad wasn't having any of it.

For nearly four days, I watched in disbelief as the house

whirled and rocked and tilted in its false happy party, and
then suddenly, everything was packed, all things were in their
places, all letters had been sent and phone calls made, and
abruptly it was the day before his departure, and I got to see
the old, familiar shadow creep across our faces. For an hour
or two of that late afternoon it was as it had always been—
Max simmering in sullen drunkenness, Harta with her legs in
the house and her head out the window in another atmosphere
entirely, and Fad with the characteristic expression on his
face of having tasted something bad and wanting to spit it
back. I wondered which of the two families would be the one
to say farewell to Fad. Would it be the old and upset family?
Or would the happy cartoon Graubarts, hand-colored by
Harta, be the ones to wave good-bye?

At dinner that night, the happy new family was clearly
in the lead. Harta cooked his favorite meal of lamb chops and
french fries, bringing out a cake with his name pricked out in
burning candles and making more speeches in the slow, deep,
undersea voice with which she'd read her poem several days
before. There was wine, which I drank some of and clandes-
tinely spit back in my glass, and a long flowery speech by
Max, too, who wound up to speed from a slow start like a car
accelerating and by the end was talking rapidly about "extended families" and "new advances" and the "the old-
fashioned toughness of the Graubart clan." In all of this, Fad
sat very still, as if frozen in space. Sometimes he rocked a
little, forward and back. The sound and light of the evening
made no more of an impression upon him than that of a wave
upon a rock.

After dinner, I went to find him where he was sitting in
his room. An orchestral piece was playing at low volume, the
wavy sound of classical music filling the air. I had been secretly dreading this moment for days. I had gone, twice, to

Harta, to complain, but each time had been told: This you have to do. "Tell him you love him. Say you'll miss him." I stepped in the door and looked at my brother. He glanced up. Glanced away.

"So, Fad," I said. "It's your big day tomorrow. How do you feel?"

"I'm going away," he said very quietly.

"Yeah, I know. How do you feel?"

"Are you?" he asked, ignoring my question.

"What?"

"Going away?"

"No."

"Where will you be?"

"When?"

"When I go."

"Away, you mean? Right here, I guess."

"Will you talk to Mommy every day?"

"Yup."

"Will you talk to Daddy every night?"

"Uh-huh."

"Will you stay in my room?"

"Sometimes, maybe."

"Oh," he said.

There was a silence. I could feel the air in the room being drawn back, back into the space around Fad's mind, like a gigantic breath.

"Fad," I said quickly, "you're going to have a great time."

For a moment, that seemed to calm him. But then he asked, "Denny? Why do I have to go away and you don't?"

"I don't know, Fad. 'Cause they say so, I guess."

"Will I grow up to be an extraspecial person?"

"Uh, yeah, sure." I said, uncertain.

"Who's the funniest boy in the world?"

Now I understood.

"You are, Fad."

"Who's the nicest child that ever was?"

"I guess that's you, right?"

"Who helps his mommy be a happy mommy?"

"You, Fad."

"And his daddy be a proud daddy?"

"You, Fad, one hundred percent."

"How come I can't cry, Denny?"

"Don't, Fad, c'mon."

"Denny," he said, "we'll be brothers forever and ever, right?"

"Yes, Fad, we will." I felt a strange lump in my throat, almost like a bruise. "Fad," I said quickly, "ya gotta understand that the point of this whole thing is to make *you* happy." This was a lie, of course, but that didn't bother me. "And it's really, truly going to be great, like, where you're going. You'll have truly lots to do, and get really healthy. Really. Just like Mommy said."

He nodded, almost imperceptibly.

"Maybe I'm scared," he said.

"Now come on," I said with Harta's voice, "you saw the place. It's a pretty place, with lots of horses—and these amazing cows."

"Maybe I'm scared, Denny." His voice began to quicken. "Denny, I don't want to be a boy who goes away."

"I know you don't, Fad. But they say you've got to. I don't like school either," I said philosophically, "but I had to start last week."

"I have to talk to Mommy."

"C'mon, Fad, not now. She's downstairs packing."

"I have to talk to Mommy," Fad said in the very same

voice, as if he hadn't heard me. "I have to talk to Mommy," he said more loudly. And then, after a moment, he shouted, "I'm getting volts!"

"Oh, Mom?" I cried, sprinting down the stairs.

The next morning, for the first time in memory, there was no organized breakfast. We simply drifted in and out of the kitchen, snagging food from the fridge on our way, and moving as if already in the aftershock of a big event. At noon, we assembled on the lawn behind a mountain of luggage. Clearly it would be the older, realer family that said good-bye, for after the raging activity of the last few days, my parents were somber, strangely quiet. Max stood with his hands in his pockets, kicking at the grass with a shoe, biting his lip and breathing heavy. Harta was holding Fad pressed up face-first against her stomach, hands crossed over his back. As I got close I heard sounds coming from her that weren't words, exactly, but something like words, a moaning, very faint beginnings of speech that seemed broadcast less from her throat and more from the center of her chest. She was shaking, too, I noticed—legs, arms, neck, and face twitching a little as if in mild electrocution, or cold, even though it was ninety degrees out and the sun was flaming directly overhead in the sky. I stood watching it all, silent. Behind my eyes was a large, high-ceilinged room filled with the fear that I wouldn't know which feelings to have and that I would, accordingly, have the wrong feelings, the very worst feelings possible, the feelings that would cause everyone to laugh out loud at me, and keep laughing till I went away and died. In an attempt to avoid this, I did the only sure thing possible. I stared, for the last time, at Fad.

He had been dressed in new, numbly cut blue flares for the occasion. He was wearing a white shirt and freshly polished shoes. His hair had been brushed back off his forehead, and his big teeth were sparkling white. You could see a lot of his teeth just then, because his mouth was drawn back to let the sobs out. He was crying hard, with a grinding, breathless sound like a hydraulic machine bent on squeezing something very small. His lashes, wet with tears, lay in ragged starbursts around his eyes and his back was shaking. Held against Harta's stomach, his nose stabbing her breastbone, he cried hard for a full minute, looking upward every few seconds, saying, "I'm going, Mommy. Mommy, I'm going away." Each time he did so, the grunting sound in Harta's chest seemed to change key, rising up one time, swooping down another.

The station wagon from Ramphill Village pulled up in front of the house and stopped. A fattish woman with cropped hair and a cap got out and said, "The Graubarts, right? You are one sight for sore eyes. What a ride up here! The traffic was backed all the way down the Garden State to Pennsylvania!"

"Oh, how sad," said Harta. "How incredibly sad."

The woman looked at her a second, surprised, and then turned back to the car to get a piece of paper, which she brought over for Max to sign. After that, she and Max opened the tailgate of the car and began loading the bags.

From several feet away, I watched myself walk over to Fad, lean forward, and hug him tight. Whiteness was in my head as I embraced him, and I smelled that strange smell coming off him of burned electrical insulation, which had always signaled his acute and uncontrollable fear. Numbness was in my mind as I watched him get in the car. I knew that big high-velocity gusts of feeling were blowing around our yard but I couldn't find them. The driver stood a moment, leaning on the open door. "You look like nice people," she said. "He'll give you a call just as soon as he arrives, alrighty?"

Fad, his face tilting from one diagonal to another, his hand in his mouth, got into the backseat of the car. The driver avoided our gazes as she shut the door after him. *Click.* Like a bolt being shot to. A sound like any other, but not this day. His face in the window was turned toward us. His lips were moving, but we couldn't hear what he said. His raised hand waved once, like a flag, and then dropped.

The car pulled out of sight down the hill. The world, having slowed for a few minutes—slowed nearly to a halt—started again with a little jolt of momentum as I swiveled my eyes and looked at Harta. She was watching the car as it receded into the distance. Piece by piece her face seemed to collapse inward, as if being sucked down some terrible drain into darkness. Then a hoarse *splat* of breath flew out of her, and suddenly she was crying, crying wildly, a broken repetitive whooping like a spanked baby, a sound I'd never heard her make before in my life. Max rushed to her, embraced her, and walked her back into the house. The screen door closed behind them with a slap. I heard her cries going on, growing softer as more doors came between her and the patch of lawn where I stood, staring into space. When my eyes dropped back to the neighborhood from the sky, I saw movement—a rash of shuttlings, shadows, twitches of drapery in a dozen picture windows. The neighbors. They'd seen the whole thing! I wanted suddenly to do something, to tell these people off unforgettably, to remind them, before they slipped back to their papers, their televisions and pot roasts and Yuban coffee, that our family was a wonderful family, a glowingly normal family, a family to be envied by all. At the moment, I contented myself with an incendiary glare with which I rifled the bay windows of our block, one by one. With the neighborhood safely in roaring flames behind me, I turned and walked slowly back inside our house.

TWENTY-FIVE

" 'Tyrannosaurus rex was the most fierce killing machine that was ever invented by Nature,' " I read out loud. " 'It was a carnosaur, which means meat-eating dinosaur, and its teeth were the approximate size and shape of bananas.' " Sudden smears of brightness interrupted my sight as my breath, in a single drawn-out *whoosh,* seemed to flee my body. Smiling by reflex, I leaned backward until the chalk trough under the blackboard bit into my spine. A cloud of fissioning soft whiteness was exploding silently in my head. I am fainting, I told myself, and tried to nod knowingly as my knees sagged, and I hung there a moment, propped up by the chalk trough. When my sight returned, accompanied by a sudden burst of hot, clinging sweat, I saw the students sitting quietly before me, a wall of fuzzy plaid and calico, praying, I was certain, for me to mess up as badly as possible. Earlier that morning, already sick with nerves, I had tried to make myself throw up by drinking some of Harta's perfume, but it hadn't done more than make me slightly nauseous, and Harta, after taking a long look at me, had insisted I go to school, "stage fright or not." Standing at the head of the class, my head slowly clearing, I burped Lanvin into my hand and began again.

" '*Tyrannosaurus rex*,' " I said and, somewhat unsteadily, began the long, grinding process of finishing the piece. I churned through the words stolen so painstakingly from the *Encyclopedia Americana*, dragging my eyes like rakes back and forth along the lines of the page. And then, suddenly, I was done. A small pattering of applause confirmed it. I was standing there with my vision still buckling slightly and my mouth open. My breath smelled funny. And Mrs. Sundifen said, "You may go back to your seat now, Denny. Good job. Any comments?"

Not long after, the bell rang to signal the end of classes for the day. I walked quickly out of the school with a feeling of enormous relief, and as I was crossing the parking lot, Sabina came up to me. My classmates were streaming past me, en route to football and cheerleader practice, music lessons and private tutors.

"I'm really sorry," she began, looking down.

I took in the distant row of trees and focused on them. "Why?"

"For the things I said the last time I spoke to you. I mean, I still think the things you said about your mother were untrue and not nice and really not Christian. But I didn't know all the unhappy things that were happening at your house."

"You mean about Fad and all?"

"Yes, Denny."

I lowered my eyes to her face. She was smiling carefully. Not too enthusiastically, but gently, her face arranged in sad attention. Smiling, she reached out and touched me on the arm. A breeze sprang up in the center of my body. I looked quickly down at the ground again. My shoes had pigeon shit on them, I noticed. I heard Sabina say, "My mother told me. It's very sad, Denny."

"Yes," I said, "I guess."

"Do you think about him?"

"Sometimes."

"Do you miss him?"

Did I miss him? I stood smiling at Sabina on the parking lot as the shapes of the other students streamed by us, and I thought of how to explain to her the old, the original problem: I didn't know. Everything to do with Fad was padded with such thick, smothering clouds of numbness that it was next to impossible to sort out my feelings. Occasionally, there was love for my brother, experienced chiefly as a desire to kill the friends who made fun of him, but most of my emotions had been scoured clean by all those years of superheated steam.

Did I miss him? I could tell Sabina that Max and Harta seemed to have drawn closer together in the wake of his departure. I could explain that I observed them each night as they sat by the flickering plum light of the television, holding hands and watching shows like Jackie Gleason and Red Skelton and occasionally laughing the kind of big billowing laughter that seemed to renovate the air around their heads, turning everything sparkling for a minute or two. But I would also have to tell her about the moments when I saw Harta put down the phone after speaking to Fad, with her face drawn and gray; when she stood with ashen shadow on her features, like she was already partly dead and sprinkled with dirt. He cried. He was lonely. He talked in a strange little pinched-off voice, like he was using only part of his throat. The people were cold and strange at Ramphill Village and they didn't sit with him for hours holding his hand like she did, stroking his hair and whispering specialness into his ear. They didn't cut his vegetables for him and write on his back at night. They wanted him to do unpleasant things like weed the garden all day, and then learn how to pick up his room, and if his back hurt or his legs ached or his throat was sore, that was just too bad.

Plus, they made him take his "meds," powerful pills that made him feel tired, washed out. I listened to Harta's long phone calls with Maude, when she sighed lots, and left such open windows of silence on the line that I felt the three of us were sitting together in a single enormous room.

"Actually," I said to Sabina, "I'm not sure."

"You're confused," said Sabina. "It's only natural. With all these things happening this summer, you've probably had quite a shock. Like when I cut my arm open to the bone and my mother had to lie in bed because her 'nerves went bad.' In fact," she said sweetly, "I'm sure you're mentally ill right now."

"You're right," I said happily.

"I want you to know," she said, "that you can talk to me about it."

"What do you mean?"

"I mean that I'm a friend, and you can talk to me about your personal stuff, like your family. The pastor of our church does 'counseling' for his parishioners. They're called his flock, like birds, and they come see him to talk about private things and it relaxes them a lot. It's a very important part of his religious, uh, vocation. You can be my flock if you want, Denny."

"Really?"

"Yes, but I have to warn you. This is very serious work, Denny."

A nearby girl called Sabina's name.

"I've gotta go!" cried Sabina, suddenly energetic. She waved good-bye and began jogging toward her friend. I stayed where I was and watched her move gracefully through the falling afternoon light, her shadow, tall and dark, running behind her across the pavement. I turned to go home. I was eager to get back to my bedroom. There was much new work to do.

During a recent routine search of Max's clothes. I had found a lipstick smudge on the collar of his jacket. When cross-referenced to Harta's collection in her handbag and medicine cabinet, it showed up as definitely coming from outside our house. Likewise the perfume I had recently caught on the monogrammed breast pocket of one of his shirts that was not one of Harta's brands. Was my father up to something? Derwent, after apologizing for his erratic behavior, had promised to show me how to read and interpret Max's Diners Club bills, and said there was a whole new world of possibility within them. A glance at my watch told me it was three-fifteen, which meant Max wouldn't be back for a whole two hours. I began to run.